Read all Books in the Lost Creek Rodeo Series

Round Up
Chute Boss
Rough Stock
Full Rigged
Half Hitch
Ace High

Chute Boss

SOPHIA SUMMERS
HEATHER B. MOORE
REBECCA CONNOLLY

KINGS ROW PRESS

Read all books by Sophia Summers

JOIN HERE for all new release announcements, giveaways and the insider scoop of books on sale.

Cowboy Inspired Series

Coming Home to Maverick

Resisting Dylan

Loving Decker

Her Billionaire Royals Series:

The Heir

The Crown

The Duke

The Duke's Brother

The Prince

The American

The Spy

The Princess

Read all the books in The Swoony Sports Romances

Hitching the Pitcher
Falling for Centerfield
Charming the Shortstop
Snatching the Catcher
Flirting with First
Kissing on Third

Vacation Billionaires
Holiday Romance

Her Billionaire Cowboys Series:

Her Billionaire Cowboy
Her Billionaire Protector
Her Billionaire in Hiding
Her Billionaire Christmas Secret
Her Billionaire to Remember

Her Love and Marriage Brides Series

The Bride's Secret
The Bride's Cowboy
The Bride's Billionaire

Chapter 1

Even though Reid Browning was born and raised outside of Washington, DC, this rodeo cowboy did not belong in a town full of suit coats anymore.

He rotated his shoulders, straining against the confining cut of the jacket he now wore. Everyone around him at the "Coming Together for Our Veterans" gala looked the same. Blue suits, ties, and short haircuts surrounded him in a stifling sea of Washington, DC lobbyists and influencers. Once a year or so, he agreed to come to something with his father, the law firm partner, the lobbyist, the schmoozer extraordinaire. And every single time, Reid was reminded why he didn't like this crowd.

He tried not to see them.

But everyone was looking at him.

Especially a table of women behind him to his right. He saw them checking him out from the corner of his eyes. They had been the whole dinner. He angled himself in his chair so that he could acknowledge them. Maybe they'd stop.

He hated to think this way about any woman, but they all seemed the same to him even though they looked different— obviously, the table was full of big hair, straight hair, classy, showy, all types. The big haired one also had more makeup than he'd seen on the rodeo queens from Lost Creek. *Not really his thing*. The blonde next to her seemed to dress with more class. She was in a tan suit, but she had her phone out, thumbs typing something while she checked him out. She took a selfie and then winked at him. *Eh*. The brunette leaned forward, a soft valley of cleavage in plain sight, and her suggestive smile said she knew it. *Moving along*. No one else stood out in any way. Not totally certain what they wanted from him, he nodded with his best cowboy smile.

No interest there. He really was beyond the days when every woman checking him out was interesting. What did they want from him? A piece of the Browning name? That's the other thing that itched his skin like a fire ant bite. Every person in this town had an agenda, and it did not include friendship and connection for the sake of being a decent human. When he looked at these women, all he saw were a bunch of opportunists.

The room was full of people just like them. Senator Harris sat at the table next to them, leaning forward, intent upon every word of the owner of the largest oil company in the country. Reid looked away. The table on their other side was full of people just trying to see and be seen. Even while talking to each other, their gazes slid around the room at everyone else.

Reid shifted in his seat, dying to take off the suit coat, but he and his father sat at the front round table, and he didn't want to draw more attention to himself.

"The redhead over there has a father who might be our

next president." Dad said the words like they might sink in somewhere in Reid. Instead, he shifted in his chair, looking away from his dad.

"Can you just sit still?" His father spoke in between smiling teeth while someone quietly took their picture. Photographers moved through the crowd, documenting the power elite. Besides his relationship to his father, Reid did not belong here. At all.

"I just think you should smile, get to know them. It certainly couldn't hurt." His dad shifted closer. "Take the redhead out tonight."

"Dad, why am I here?"

"To meet people. If you want to move up in the world, you have to know some of these players, show up now and then."

Reid didn't want to move up in the world of lawyers and lobbyists. "That's why I do rodeo." He almost tipped his hat, except he wasn't wearing it. And that made him stretch his neck against his tie. Any event that was unfriendly to cowboy hats was unfriendly to him.

"Pay attention to this next speaker. She has a lot of influence on the Hill right now."

His father dismissed rodeo like he had Reid's two-year degree. No matter he'd won the collegiate championship in bareback. That little part of Reid's history was swept under his father's rug. All that mattered to the man was Reid's law degree and his time at Harvard the four years before that. He sat taller. Well, he didn't do rodeo to impress his father so what did it matter? His gaze wandered. The new speaker's voice washed over him like soft sheets. It was nice, mellow, comfortable sounding. He didn't care what she was saying, but the sound was putting him to sleep. As his eyes closed, Dad's foot kicked his shin.

"Don't fall asleep."

Wincing inside, but keeping his face "Browning polite," he locked eyes with his dad. "I'm finished here."

"No you're not. I need you to meet Miss Cooper and then talk to the publicity team about getting you on the board of her non-profit."

He didn't groan, but he felt like he was in high school all over again. What he really wanted was to get back up on his horse. "Who is Miss Cooper?"

His dad indicated their speaker. So Reid looked at her for the first time. Wow. He nodded. Now here was something interesting. Her blonde hair fell in waves, the kind that shifted across her shoulders whenever she turned her head. Hands rested comfortably on the podium while she spoke. She was a natural up there. The crowd laughed at something she said, and her face lit with a stunning smile. The podium was angled so that he could see the little bounce in her foot while she talked. She looked like a runner, strong. She was small, but he bet she could wrestle her own steer if she wanted to. Who was she again? He checked the program. Ah, the head of the non-profit his father wanted him to support. His gaze slid over her again. He had no problem meeting a beautiful woman who was smart and interesting.

His father's eyes were too knowing. He no doubt hoped a pretty face would bring Reid out to DC more. Reid didn't say more about meeting her or helping on the board, but he didn't say more about leaving, either.

When he turned back to Miss Cooper, her attention had shifted to him, unfortunately catching him with his head turned. Her gaze lingered for a minute, but she glossed over him as though he didn't matter and looked out over the room to say her next words. "Every bit helps vets struggling from neuro-related injuries sustained in battle."

Ah, *more interesting*. A cause he could get behind, led by a stunning woman. His lips curled, just at the corners.

"Did you know that the number one highest demographic of homeless people in our country are women veterans? These men and women signed up and went, risked everything to do what was asked for their country. And we are finding out that the negative health consequences are far more lasting than we would have ever predicted. When every person in this room benefits from their service, it seems a natural response to want to care for them. We could use your help." Her whole face lit with the passion behind her words. "How often have you driven across state lines in this country without giving it a second thought? How often have you ever been worried for your lives? Those are freedoms preserved by men and women willing to lay down *their* lives to protect them." Her words were on fire, carrying out across a silent room. She had stopped checking her notes. Passion seeped out of her skin or something. It expanded around her, as if the air shimmered. Reid was caught up in her words. His smile grew. The whole picture of this spit fire of a woman standing up in the front of everyone was suddenly making what used to be a waste of an afternoon all that more worthwhile.

Selfie Woman was on her feet for some reason. She breezed closer to him, nudging his shoulder, but then dropped something near his chair. A cell phone? He reached for it and then looked to find its owner. Her perfume was stronger than he liked and she was suddenly close enough that he knew it.

"Thank you," she whispered, leaning forward so he got a full view of the contents of her shirt and forgive him, but he did not need those in his head. He looked away, forcing his eyes back up into her face.

"Aren't you a gentleman." Her whispers were closer to his ear this time and sent bumps down his neck, which her finger traced as she stood.

No way, lady. He nodded, once, briefly, and then directed his attention back to the speaker, who'd unfortunately caught the whole interchange. Selfie Woman's hand rested on the top of his shoulder before she moved away. He wanted nothing more than to shrug off her touch, but that wouldn't be gentlemanly. He just had no interest. And he wanted Miss Cooper to respect him. He couldn't explain why, but there it was. Something about the woman up in front screamed "real deal."

His father cleared his throat.

Reid stretched his legs out underneath the table but bumped the person across from them. Trying to cram ten people into these banquet rounds just wasn't working for his six-foot-four wide frame. His father's glare underneath the Browning polite mask was itching to be challenged. And Reid was more bored than he'd ever been, beautiful woman aside. He'd come. He'd supported his dad. He was done. Miss Cooper ended her speech, and everyone clapped.

She returned to her seat, which was up on the podium area directly in front of him.

The master of ceremonies stood again. "In honor of Miss Cooper's service in Iraq, we invite you all to stand for the Pledge of Allegiance and national anthem."

His jaw nearly dropped to the floor. *That little lady had served?* His gaze returned to her place on the stand. She sent not even a flicker of attention his way. Then they stood, his hand reverently found his heart and he recited with the room, "I pledge allegiance, to the flag of the United States of America and to the republic for which it stands, one nation under God indivisible with liberty and justice for all."

The silence following the pledge filled the room, but was not exactly the reverent kind he'd have appreciated. Then a voice started singing the national anthem, and he closed his eyes. Some moments were sacred and deserved to be treated as such. The words to their country's national anthem meant something to him. And to rodeo in general.

They had a few more remarks, another call for money, a reminder about an online auction, and way too many other details. When at last everything was finished, he stood next to his father, shaking hands with a million heads. A million faces he would never remember again.

Until hers.

Miss Cooper approached them but with smiles only for his father.

"And Eden Cooper. Important words you shared today." His father covered her hand with his own. "Thank you for the work you do." Was he almost tender with this woman?

"I'm so pleased to do it. When you've experienced the things I have, the next step is to help with the solutions."

"Have you met my son?"

She nodded. "Yes, Reid. It's good to see you again." Her eyes challenged him. And something sparkled with familiarity, but how did he know this woman? How could he ever forget such a face?

"You as well." He reached out his hand.

Her face flashed with disappointment. "That's too bad."

"Pardon me?" His hand remained outstretched until it was obvious she was not going to clasp it.

"We've never met. I wondered what you'd do if I claimed an association."

Irritation brewed. Claiming association happened all the time in this know-and-be-known town. "Hedging for a moment to spare your feelings while I try to remember who you are is … normal. Everybody does that."

"Better to acknowledge straight up we have never met."

"What if we had and I couldn't remember? It's much more polite to play along for a minute. No one wants to be forgotten."

"But no one wants to be strung along, either." Her eyes sharpened.

His father tensed beside him, and Reid knew the best thing would be to just play along with whatever little game this was. He pressed his mouth together and then dipped his head. "Excellent point. I will take that to heart next time someone tries to trick me during our introduction." He just had to be polite for ten more seconds then he was out of there.

"Touché," she acknowledged. "Perhaps it was a bit too bold. I assumed you could handle it."

"Oh, I can handle just about anything you—"

"My son is here at my request to talk about accepting that position on the board on behalf of Browning LLC. He has a great respect for the cause of veterans and caring for them."

Reid bit back his retort and nodded. "Certainly. I do indeed have a huge respect for the cause. And I'd be happy to serve on the board. I'm not often in town but I will do what I can. Shall we be in touch about my specific duties?"

"I'm sure the chairman of the board will reach out. His name is Nigel Fensteen." She turned to his father. "Thank you for your support. Having your firm and name involved will make all the difference."

"Anything we can do." His father smiled the supportive expression Reid had rarely received from him and then Miss Cooper moved on.

His father's face was blank, his voice, low. "Did you have to argue with the woman?"

"What are you talking about? She was ridiculous. Who does that? Tries to trick a person at their first meeting?"

"It doesn't matter. We smooth over the awkward not amplify it."

"What is this we? *We* don't do anything. Is this a new family motto?" Reid was having a really tough time hiding his irritation. "Look. I've gotta go."

His father's sigh grated further. "Yes, you've graced us long enough."

"Thank you." He turned and almost stumbled over Selfie Woman. "Excuse me." His arms went out to steady her and she melted closer. "And where are you going?" She pouted up into his face.

"You tell me." She'd be an easy way out the front door at least. He held out his arm and almost cringed as her giggling form clung to him.

"Should we invite your friends?" He paused at their table. "Where is the fun happening this evening?" He'd already decided this group was not for him; give them some friends for each other, and he was out.

About half of them stood, joining him. He left the room without another glance over his shoulder.

Big Hair attached herself to his other arm, and he regretted his company the minute he stepped out of the ballroom. "Let's go get margaritas." She giggled.

"Oh yes." Brunette stopped walking right in front of his

chest. They would have run into her if he hadn't forced an awkward stop. The others crowded in and the laughing energy might have been intriguing a few years ago, might even have been fun in Lost Creek with the good people of that small town, but here, it just grated.

Everyone else seemed to be in agreement with the call for margaritas, and since he was not, he waited with them for the Ubers to get there. He opened the first door and Brunette and Big Hair slid in, no doubt expecting him to follow, but he closed the door. He did the same for the next car, then waved at their receding bumpers from the curb, laughing in anticipation at their surprise when they pulled up to the Blue Lagoon and he hadn't joined them. As soon as their cars were out of sight, he took off his suit coat, rolled up his sleeves, loosened and then ripped off his tie. One good thing about this evening that he could think of? He would be heading back home to Texas tomorrow evening.

Chapter 2

Eden joined her parents in their Virginia home.

"You were wonderful up there, honey." Her mother's comforting tones that used to ease all that was wrong in the world, just didn't work the same as they had when she was a kid. For one, something about her expression made Eden suspect that perhaps she was not pleased after all. She sighed. "Thank you, Mom. I'm doing my best. Hopefully we'll get some donations out of it." Did her mom really think she'd done an excellent job or was she about to segue into some finer points of improvement?

"And new seats on the board, right?" Her eyes widened too innocently

Eden bristled. "Yes. That too."

"Who was that handsome man? Is he Mr. Browning's son?" She glistened, literally turned glow-y, whenever Eden talked about a man.

"I did meet Mr. Browning's son." *Unfortunately.* "He's the one who will be serving on the board from the Browning Trust."

"Oh, I like him." Her smile and approval were ridiculous. She'd never met him. And knew only that he was good looking. But Eden had come to suspect that she was incredibly shallow in her assessments of men. Thank the heavens she'd married Eden's father.

"I'm not sure I'll see him much. I get the impression he's in Texas a lot."

Her father leaned forward. "Oh?"

"Oh right. So you guys might see him more than I will." She laughed. Because obviously Texas was huge. "When are you moving to Lost Creek permanently?"

"We just decided this weekend that we're ready. But the house isn't. At least the caretakers and Bear are enjoying the big Texas skies while we wait here. It's time we dig into our retirement."

Bear. Man, she missed her dog. That huge Newfoundland was probably having the time of his life out in Texas, but she wished she'd been able to keep him with her in Arlington.

"She's serious. This ranch will give your mother plenty to do, that's for sure."

"And the people? Have you guys liked visiting this town?"

"Oh sure. Honey, they're just like you hear about small towns. Everyone knows everyone and there are some really decent people there doing good by each other and we are excited to rub shoulders with them all."

"That's great." She was happy for her parents, but her head was really starting to pound. She lifted a hand to her temple.

"Another headache?" Her father eyed her closely.

"Yeah. I'm sure it will go away by tomorrow. It's been a big day. I knew it was coming." She got headaches now.

One of her thank you gifts from Iraq. The other being multiple concussions and emotional damage, and a growing pile of tests showing possible neurological damage.

Her mom frowned. "But maybe there's a solution for all this. Maybe we could see another specialist or something."

"They're working on it, Mom. All this trauma response to explosions is sort of new. What I have is concussion damage from it."

They sat in her parents' cozy living room, in the house of her childhood. It would become her house. She sunk into their couch. "Maybe I'll get some sleep."

Something passed between her parents, a…look.

She closed her eyes and counted in her head. They were about to mention something…an intervention? The start of a heart-to-heart? A different form of treatment?

"We've been thinking."

"Oh yeah?"

"Yes." Her father's voice was firm. Kind, but settled.

Eden opened her eyes.

"I just recently heard about a ranch out in Lost Creek."

What on earth would this conversation have to do with her? "A…ranch?"

"People spend time there, as much as they need, and a highly regarded woman runs it. She's the therapist."

Eden moaned.

"And other women come. It's for up to 30 days…"

"Thirty days! Are you guys like, admitting me or something?"

"No, of course not. But we've met the woman, Kellie Prosper, and she's a real special person. When I started talking to her about what she does, I just knew she could be helpful to you."

What's it called?"

"Broken Hearts Ranch."

Eden shook her head. "But I don't have a broken heart." What was this? A bunch of women thwarted in love?

"No, you've got a broken head. That's even worse." Trust her father to really point out the logical issue.

"It's not at all." Though she had no idea. She'd never had a broken heart.

"But honey. I think your heart's been bruised as well from all the stuff you had to see over there."

"Over there." That's about as far as her mother went in wanting to discuss what went on 'over there' while she served in Iraq.

Her father nodded as though he'd figured out her cure. As though it were that simple. "I think you could give this woman and her ranch a try. Go while Congress is not in session. Go get yourself all fixed up."

Eden smiled. Maybe she would. Maybe not. But she didn't really want to talk about it any more. "I'll take a look, Dad. Maybe it will be just the thing to get me all *fixed up*."

He patted her hand. "That's a girl."

"Now tell me more about your dating life." Her mom meant well. Goodness she did. But lately it seemed like she asked all the wrong questions.

And with that one question, Eden was all but convinced to go give the ranch a try, if only to get herself out of DC. She sighed. "None of the guys I meet seem like…keepers." She shrugged. "They're crazy flirts. Or like that guy today for example—say all kinds of things they don't mean. You don't know who you're really talking to. And walking out with women all over him." She hissed. "It's embarrassing for him, really, and do I want to be one more on his arm? I certainly do not." She frowned. "He's probably the kind of guy that is a different person to everybody he meets, you know? Knows how to play the game?"

"Are we talking about somebody specific here?" her dad's eyes twinkled at her.

"Not at all. Well, that one Browning guy, but he's just like all the others. That's what I mean. I don't date much, Mom. They just don't have that solid goodness that says, 'this is gonna last.'"

"Well, I can understand that. And don't you settle."

They had reached the point where every dating conversation ended. "I won't, Mom. Don't you worry about that."

"I won't, I just want you to be happy. I don't like to think of you lonely."

"Maybe I need to get myself all fixed up before I can date someone anyway."

"Give that nice ranch lady a call." Her mother stood. "I think I need some early sleep too." She leaned down to kiss Eden on the cheek. "Good night, love."

"Good night."

Her parents walked up the stairs a little more slowly than they ever had. She was happy to spend the night, especially after they'd made such an effort to come to Arlington and hear her speak. But now, she missed her apartment, her view, and her…solitude.

She pulled out her laptop and typed, "Broken Hearts Ranch."

A simple looking website pulled up. Organized, crisp, straightforward. She liked it. And without meaning to, she dug deeper, encouraged by everything she saw. A person could opt to stay for as long or as little as they wished, up to a month. Insurance did cover costs, but they were adamant about scholarships, if needed, and as she scrolled to the bottom, she saw a stamp that intrigued her. "Wounded Warrior approved."

So did they have knowledge or experience talking to vets? She scrolled some more. The schedule was lovely. The land in the pictures was beautiful and expansive. And she liked that there was a real working ranch as a part of things. Did she see herself bringing in the cows? Probably not. But a good horse ride in the evenings sounded heavenly.

She clicked over to her calendar. A solid month stretched out where everything kind of shut down. She could work on her non-profit in the down time, but she had a board of directors for that. She snorted. And a new guy who'd just promised to help out.

With a smile, she clicked on admissions. Now, if they had an opening, she would see if she could get in. The thought of leaving all the guys—like that creep Reid—behind, and maybe meeting some real cowboys, some good men, and the women at the ranch, talking to new fresh people, relaxing in the hammocks…All of a sudden it sounded like the very vacation she'd been waiting for. Her parents still knew a thing or two, didn't they?

Registration completed, hoping for a spot for twenty days in Broken Hearts Ranch. She sent all instructions, directions and welcome information to her email, closed her laptop and jumped in the shower. This would be great for her. She was convinced. Her mind spun with all the opportunities, and most of all, the break. She turned off the water and realized her headache had gone away.

Chapter 3

Since Reid was going to be leaving that evening to go back to Texas, he took his morning run at the Mall downtown. He'd biked in from the Langley area where his parents lived and then chained the bike up while he started doing his laps. Eden Cooper worked downtown, didn't she? He tried to put dumb questions out of his mind. Why was he thinking about Eden?

He loved the Mall area. He loved the monuments. He could sit and stare up into Jefferson's face all day, or Lincoln's, or Roosevelt's. He could sit back on a bench and stare at the highest point of the Washington Monument, thinking about George Washington, thinking about Hamilton and his wife who commissioned it to be built. But he could not stand what happened on what they called "The Hill." The lobbyists, the special interest groups, the political parties, all of it. He'd had his fill being around a father who was completely caught up in it all.

So today, as he ran past the trees that would blossom

into an enchanting pink in about one month's time, he celebrated what was good about his country.

His phone buzzed. A quick glance told him he might want to slow to a walk for this. The Chute, his texting group from the guys, his rodeo brothers, or at least that's what they were to him. It was useful during competition to be able to talk to the whole team. And so they'd created The Chute. But it stuck and now he felt like they were a part of his daily life, more or less. What had them all razzed now? His phone was buzzing like crazy from his waist pocket.

He slowed to a walk, but then thought it'd be better to just sit on the nearest bench. Westin was going on about some raccoon that was trying to bunk down with him under his truck in the middle of the night.

Reid started to laugh and he kept going until he had tears. *Dude. Why don't you sleep in the truck bed?*

I told you. I like having something over my head.

Like a roof? Reid could almost see Eric shaking his head.

Westin continued. *Anyway, you rude cusses are interrupting a good story. So something starts breathing.*

A lot of emojis followed that statement.

And it's breathing close. And I'm ready to shoot the dang thing, but then it plops down next to me and goes to sleep.

No! Reid didn't believe his junk for one minute.

Sure as I'm living clean.

What did you do? Ford was buying this? Nah, he was playing along.

I was so tired I fell asleep too.

Reid's stomach hurt from the laughs that tugged at his insides. Joggers looked at him like he was half crazy. He took a picture of himself and sent it. *I'm dying.*

You downtown?

Yep

Ain't you coming to Texas? Lars got to the point. Right where they should be.

Sure as there are no blossoms on these trees, I'm coming back today. We got a rodeo to run.

You hear that? The boss is coming back. Better warn the REAL chute boss.

Very funny. If that guy would learn to cinch my horse at the right time.

Yeah, we know. He knows. Everybody knows.

It was no secret how frustrated Reid was when someone couldn't get their job right. Ryan had been thinking about stepping in. It was time.

If Ryan just took over, things would be better. Ryan knows when the animal needs to be cinched.

Conversation drifted to rodeo and animals and the calves. More often than not they were talking about the animals. And why not? They were the lifeblood of the rodeo. People thought it was he and the guys and gals that ran the show, but really, he tipped his hat to the animals. So much depended on them and most people didn't even know it.

Heads up. Kellie says we have a new group of women coming in and we're to leave them alone for a bit, or forever, depending.

Which is it? A bit or forever?

We're supposed to go at their pace and not try anything permanent.

A whole bunch of thumbs up followed that announcement. Most of the guys didn't want to get involved over there anyway. The women were struggling. They had healing in their future, sometimes real deep hurt. And he for one, would only get in the way.

A runner caught his attention. *Eden Cooper.* How in tarnation was she there? He stood, ready to move, but he didn't really know why except it had suddenly become important to have some more time with the woman. Maybe he didn't like it that he'd left things the way he had.

Gotta run.

What? We are not finished here.

Bet he just saw a beautiful woman.

Take a picture of her.

When he didn't respond, Ryan made him laugh by asking, *Do you think we'll ever know?*

Nah. Reid's a locked safe. And we don't have that combination.

He sent a laughing emoji, then pocketed the phone while he took off running. Eden kept an insane pace. He might catch her, but as his legs pounded into the packed dirt beneath his feet, he realized he might die first.

As he got closer, the idiocy of his actions sort of hit all at once. *Why was he doing this?*

He had no idea. He didn't like this woman, did he? Thinking of his last interaction with her, he shook his head. No, he did not. His feet kept moving toward her. There was something there, some itch, some…thing that he couldn't figure out. And like a stupid moth drawn to a bug zapper, he seemed doomed to figure out just what it was that had him spellbound. Really? *Spellbound*? Nah, but running at this insane pace around the water toward the Lincoln Memorial had to mean something.

He got nearer but kept his distance, mostly because he was breathing so hard she might think cardiac arrest was imminent. He might think so too. Dang. Before this sprint around the Tidal Basin, he had thought he was in great shape.

She ran right on past the Jefferson. He groaned. No breaks.

Her head turned slightly toward him, but then faced the front again.

Should he call out to her? Get her to stop? Before he could do something so foolish, he bit his tongue. He had nothing to say to the woman. Not a thing. He forced his feet to stop moving, his lungs gasping for air, then he turned around and started walking back in the direction from which he'd come.

Whatever had gotten into him, it was nothing a good ride on his horse Sundance couldn't fix. Then a heavy ride on a bareback bronc would do the trick to shake it out of his system. He used his shirt to wipe his face and then realized he was one big sweaty mess. He pulled it off and used it to rub his head all over, his face, chest, and arms. A light breeze picked up, and he welcomed the crispness to the air. March in Washington, DC was not spring like in other places, more like lingering cold icy winter. But after a run like that, he was plenty hot anyway. He paused at the pull-up bar. Someone had added these challenges and fitness areas to quite a few walking and running paths in DC and northern Virginia. His hands lifted him up to the bar with ease, the first time. He crossed his legs at the ankles and began pull ups, one after another after another.

The sweat returned, but the breeze chilled him and he kept on going. "Forty-one. Forty-two." Something about pushing himself, burning his muscles, continuing past his ability felt great right now. Eden kept coming to mind. He'd thrust her out with the next pull of his arms, but right back she'd come. Her ridiculous test, her accusatory smirk, her knowing smile. He couldn't stand when people assumed things about him. Labels. Hated those too. And she was throwing all kinds of assumptions, and likely labels too. She didn't know him at all. His arms were getting tired. "Fifty-five." He rose slowly. "Fifty-six." He hung for a moment, made a decision, and then pushed through to "Sixty." His breath came out hard. He stopped, grabbed his shirt, and wiped himself down again.

He better get back. And now he was going to be sore for his practice tomorrow in Texas. He rotated his arms, stretching his shoulders while he walked back toward the Mall area and to where he'd left his bike. His frustration had eased, but his body was feeling it.

His feet sluggishly carried on. After about five minutes, the sounds of running footsteps approached. He hardly noticed until Eden passed him.

"Couldn't keep up?" Eden called back over her shoulder and ran right on by, as quickly as she had before. Was she a machine?

Every part of him bristled. And a new energy surged up inside. No way was she just gonna run by leaving challenges like that around. Even though every part of his body complained, he started at a run, determined to catch Eden Cooper, pass her, and not look back. *Couldn't keep up*, she said. Right. He could keep up. He pushed harder, his legs stretching, his lungs feeling like they might split. And Eden grew closer.

And closer. Was she even tired? As far as he could tell, no. Just well-paced, moving along, her muscles tight, her arms in rhythm. She made running look good, he'd give her that. But he was tired of her attitude, or something.

He was close enough to see the sweat glistening on the back of her neck, soaking just a bit into her shirt on her back. She was beautiful. But he didn't stop. He pounded into the hard packed dirt, pushing ever harder. Exhilaration filled his lungs, which hurt with each intake, as he was ready to pass on by. Her foot caught a dip, or something, but it caused her to lose her balance and she stumbled, legs flailing.

His feet got caught in hers. While desperately trying to stay upright, he stumbled forward, shoving into her which meant for sure she was going down. Giving up on keeping his balance, he pulled her close and shifted his body so that his shoulder hit first, sliding along in the dirt with her on top of him.

They stopped, a dust cloud billowing up all around them. He coughed. His nose itched, but he couldn't reach his face.

She scrambled to rise up off of him. Her legs were all scratched up from the road burn. He could only guess what he looked like. Everything hurt, muscles and now the sting of skin scrapes. But he couldn't tell if that was just because he'd been running like an idiot or if it was from slamming onto the ground with a surprisingly heavy Eden on top of him.

Her hands brushed at her clothes for a moment and then gave up. At last she looked at him. "Are you all right?"

He groaned. "I think so." As he sat, his shoulder was stiff, and his skin stung like the devil. But everything worked.

"Bet you wish you'd just kept your shirt on." Her tone was...indecipherable. Did she have opinions about him taking off his shirt on a run? He'd about had it with this woman and all her opinions. But he held his tongue.

"Am I bleeding?" He turned so she could see his shoulder and back.

She hissed. "Ouch."

He waited.

"No blood yet. But it's caked in this dirt, rock stuff we've been running in. Do you want me to wash it out?" She held up her water bottle.

He considered her. Then shook his head. "Nope. I think I'll just wash it out when I get home."

"Okay…can I do something? Help?"

"Nope. Definitely not that." He tried to stretch his arm, but winced. Yep, this was gonna be an issue at the competition next week. He about growled to the universe, but instead just turned to hobble away. His bike was on the next block.

"Let me drive you. This is crazy. You need to see yourself."

He waved a hand back over his shoulder. "I got it. Just go back to work."

"I'm off. I'm taking the break between sessions off."

He didn't answer. None of this mattered to him. Right now, he just wanted to get home, take a shower, and assess the damage.

"I have time to take you wherever you need to go."

He turned. "And my bike?"

"Oh, well."

"Right. So I think I'll do what I said I was gonna do, which is take my bike home."

Her eyes dimmed with hurt and he almost regretted his tone, but his skin was starting to itch and sting at the same time. He started walking again.

She said nothing but he could hear her footsteps behind him. Dang that woman. Go away.

Kneeling to unlock his bike shot knife-like points of pain through him. But soon he was standing again, the lock was stored away, and he walked the bike to the sidewalk. He'd take Highway One and ride along the river to Langley. It was still a good ten miles away, but the ride was nice and easy, and flat for the most part. He could make it. Nothing like riding bareback.

But Eden stuck with him. He straddled his bike, put a foot on the pedal and then turned to her again. "Do you need help?"

"No. My car is over there." Her leg was starting to bleed, the dirt soaking in the red of her blood.

"Are you gonna be able to wash that?"

"Yeah. I'll be fine. I'll just take care of it at home." She looked like she wanted to say more. He could almost feel the urge growing inside.

"Just say it." He gritted his teeth. The longer he stood still, the more he wanted to get moving.

"I just…I'm sorry. And…thank you for catching my fall."

He studied her face. Those had not been easy words to say. "You're all right, Eden." He tipped his imaginary hat and then hopped on his bike to ride away. With any luck, he'd never see that woman again.

Chapter 4

Eden limped back to her car. She hadn't wanted to let on, but her ankle was killing her.

She guzzled the last of her water bottle.

What had gotten into her? Did she have to keep up the pace of death just because Reid was around? If her legs hadn't felt like Jell-O on that last stretch, she wouldn't have stumbled, he wouldn't have been tripped up, and they wouldn't have gone down together.

Wow, his road burn was gonna be rough. When he saw it, he might really hate her.

Which was fine.

She wasn't into him either, but now she couldn't just be irritated. Now she was at fault. She hated this feeling. Should she call him to check on him?

"No." Was this part of her emotional condition? Feeling responsible for everyone and everything in her life? This guilt? Some kind of co-dependent addiction? She didn't know. Maybe she should get some more therapy. What she really wanted was to feel normal. But she was afraid that wasn't an option, at least not right away.

Perhaps Kellie and the Broken Hearts Ranch could give her a springboard back into a healthy life again. Heaven knows she'd need her brain when Congress went back in session. They had some bills to fight that were about to be introduced on the floor and some she'd like to see pass.

Her chest started to tighten again. Her hands had been shaking, her legs wobbly from exertion, but this tightening, this was her old friend, anxiety. Thoughts of the coming months were just compounding her angst about leaving. Maybe she should cancel the whole trip and get started on some of that work.

She closed her eyes. It was so much easier not to do anything. Her leg stung and the throbbing increased as she climbed into her car. On the drive home, she vacillated between staying home and going four times. After she'd showered and sat on her couch with bandages and ice, she opened her laptop and pulled up the ranch's website again. Were there any reviews anywhere?

She did a random google search and a Facebook search. People were pretty close lipped about this place. Probably a good thing if everyone was recovering from heartbreak. What would the group counseling be like? How many women there could relate to her situation?

After thinking about it for the hundredth time, she checked the timing of her flight and knew that she was all checked in. She was packed. It was paid for. She was gonna go. She'd try it out, and then if it wasn't working, she'd just hightail it back to Virginia early. Thinking about her painful morning and afternoon, she had to recognize that if leaving meant avoiding men like Reid, then she was all for a nice break. She loved her job, her life, but dealing with some of the power brokers got a bit old. Not a bit, a lot.

Reid's smug face at the dinner, while the women fawned over him. Watching him walk out of the event hall with one on each arm, surrounded by a mass of estrogen. She shook her head. Nope. And if he was going to start working on Vets 4 Life, she'd just as soon avoid the board meetings altogether. Her decision made, she finished packing a few odds and ends, refreshed the ice on her ankle, and then fell asleep with her foot elevated on two pillows.

The next morning, spurred by alternating feels of guilt for Reid's road burn and irritation at his arrogant player ways, she grabbed a taxi to the airport and was on a plane to Texas before she could change her mind.

The San Antonio airport was everything she expected Texas to be. Pictures of the rolling hill country, dotted with long horn cows, filled the wall space. Large roller coasters and Shamu, the whale, filled other places. There were stores that sold cowboy hats and Ariat boots—she even saw some prickly pear cactus jelly for sale. Halfway through the terminal, she came to a crossroad of hallways and an open area where their second floor could look down on the first. Loud cheering drew her attention and she paused to look over the edge.

Everyone was clapping, cheering, and had stopped what they were doing to face one direction. She peered over the edge, but couldn't make out what was causing the commotion. Maybe she'd happened upon the Spurs coming home from a game or something. She was about to give up and keep walking, even though the cheering continued, until someone in military khakis came into view.

Her heart leapt to her throat. Had a group of soldiers come home? They at last came into view, a whole group of them, twenty or more, and she joined her clapping to the others. Tears filled her eyes. Why did she want to cry? For her own tour of duty? For theirs? In gratitude? In the vicarious receipt of such an outpouring of support? She didn't know, but something inside was touched, deeply, and she couldn't clap loudly enough.

They soon passed out of sight, but the cheering followed them, down further on that level. She started walking again in the direction of the exit. She wiped at her eyes. Wow, she was a mess, right? Was this normal? Going to Broken Hearts ranch might be a great idea after all.

She waved at her Uber driver, and was soon on her way through the crowded streets near the airport and out into the country. At least she would get to see Bear. She missed that dog. Moving to Northern Virginia and working her schedule had meant leaving the dog with her parents. They had been good sports. But Bear was large by any standard. Huge. But such a love. His big eyes loving on you and holding you in their gaze with the adoration of a puppy. She could use a little of that in her life too.

At last, the Uber arrived at her parents' ranch. They were still building and fixing it up, but a few rooms were finished, and they went back and forth between the bed and breakfast in town and the new house. They weren't there at the moment, but apparently Bear was.

She whistled and asked the driver to wait.

Bear came leaping toward them.

"What is that thing?" The driver inched the car forward even though her door was still open.

"He's my dog. He's the biggest softy you'll ever see."

"I'm not so sure about that."

"No really. He's great. Besides, the drive from here to

the ranch is just another three minutes down the road, right?"

"Whoa, no way. That dog is not getting in this car."

Bear leapt past Eden and climbed into the back seat.

"Lady, no. No. I don't allow dogs. Of any size, but especially not this one."

Bear licked the back of his head.

"Really? And I don't do dog slime either."

"Oh, he doesn't slobber." *Much.* "He'll be so good. Sit."

Bear promptly sat. He must have sensed that his time with Eden was coming to a close unless he behaved.

"I'll double your fare."

The driver didn't think twice. "Done."

She closed the door and he took off, a bit faster than Eden felt was necessary, but it would do the trick. She pushed the tip button and paid the guy the cost of the complete fare in tip and then clicked send. "I'll leave you a fabulous review too."

"I appreciate it." He didn't look like he appreciated anything about this trip, but they should be almost there.

He pulled into a long drive, under a metal sign that read "Broken Hearts Ranch." The drive was lined with crepe myrtle trees. Pink blossoms were just starting to bloom. This would be magical in just a few days. The stretch of green grass from the entrance to the front door was so beautiful. Two live oaks with massive branches filled the space closer to the house, and farther back, white rail fences divided the horses from the rest of the property. A tall red barn, opened, nestled back toward the woods of the property. "It's rustic."

He didn't answer but pulled in the semi-circle drive in front of the house. "Here you go."

She opened the door and Bear tore out. "Bear, come."

He stopped and shocked her by returning to her side. "Good dog. Sit."

Then he sat, to her shock and amazement. "Has someone been training you?" She pat his head. The driver set her luggage at her feet.

"Thank you."

He nodded, hopped in his car, and drove out of there like his trunk was on fire.

For a moment, she just drank in the air. It was nice—a bit of a chill tickled her skin—but warm. The sun felt comforting. And she was happy for the light sweater. She tugged at the rolling luggage and put the duffle on her shoulder while she walked up the sidewalk. It felt…odd, to be moving into a place she had never been, with plans to stay there for three weeks. Her chest started to tighten. Her body was working up something to stress over. She felt it in her shoulders as well. But, she reminded herself, she could leave whenever she liked. She could leave right now if she wanted. Bear nudged her. Probably sensed her crazy tension.

Concentrated breathing brought her up the front steps and helped her feel more in control of her situation. And then the door opened to such a kind face that some of her tension left with her next breath. Maybe she would be okay at this ranch.

"Eden Cooper?" The friendly woman with blonde hair, the same color as Eden's, smiled into Eden's face.

"Yes, hi, I'm Eden."

"It's so good to meet you. I'm Kellie Prosper. You've come to the right place." The surety with which she spoke those words sank deep into Eden's worry and dispersed more of the tightness.

"Thank you." She exhaled slowly.

"And who is this?" She bent down to hold her hand out to Bear. Though she didn't have to bend too far. The dog filled the space on the front porch.

"This is Bear. The registration process said we could bring our pets?"

"Of course. We're happy to have him. This is a working ranch and we have plenty of land to keep him happy. Does he sleep with you? In a crate? Outside?"

Eden couldn't be certain, but there might have been a hopeful lift to the word, outside. She laughed. "Bear is happy outside. In your barn. Or he'll sleep at the foot of my bed on the floor."

Kellie considered him. "I'll let you settle in and take a look at the barn or garage. You can decide."

"Thank you." Really, that was super kind. As seen by the Uber driver, most people had a problem with Bear. He was just too big to be a comfortable guest. But he sure helped Eden. She'd missed him in DC. But obviously the mammoth could not sleep in her apartment, nor would he be happy all alone most of the time while she worked.

She was grateful she could sleep the first night with him in her room. Maybe he could sleep outside after tonight. After she got used to the room. They didn't come as often now, but nightmares would probably stay with her for the rest of her life, if what the therapists had all said was true. When Bear was there, she could stem the worst of them by just reaching for her dog. But in Virginia, she'd gotten to the point where she was only having one a month or so. And that was livable. Everything about her conditions was livable. She could handle the anxiety. She could handle the fuzzy brain, though sometimes it got so bad she lost her train of thought mid-sentence. She'd prayed and prayed it wouldn't happen in her speech. All the important phrases and sentences she had written out. Teleprompters freaked her out. What if they failed? She much preferred the handwritten paper as backup.

While Eden's thoughts were a jumble of confusion, moving forward and backward in time, she and Bear followed Kellie back into the house.

"Our front room. Plenty of games and books and blankets in the storage benches. The kitchen. Open most hours if you want to cook for yourself. But we serve up three meals a day on rotation, taking turns, and I think you'll like what our cook creates in here, when we have a cook." As she went through room by room, Eden waited for her anxiety to amp back up, for her to be worried about any number of things, but it never did. Not yet anyway.

"How long have you lived here?"

"For a long time, seems like. This was my family home, and after my divorce, I decided to move back and with my brother Ryan's help, turn it into a recovery center."

"Ryan?" Something about a man around didn't sit well with her.

"There's a house on the property he lives in. Comes by to help out and serves as a ranch hand. This is a real running ranch with all kinds of work happening around you ladies."

"How many are here right now?"

"We got four of you now, and a whole slew coming in next week. Our capacity is ten, but we rarely have that many."

She entered a bright room with yellow curtains, a comfortable looking bed, a dresser, and a large closet. "This is lovely."

"I'm glad you like it. I figured after serving in the military, anything might feel like comfort."

She laughed. "That's true. But I don't often see anything like what I slept in over there."

"I bet that's true." Kellie smiled another one of her genuine smiles. "We're proud to have you stay with us. You'll find we're a patriotic group and are honored to give back a little to someone who has already given so much."

She never knew what to do or say when people got all sentimental about her time in Iraq. "Thank you."

"There's a welcome packet right there on your dresser. It has all the talks with me on there scheduled for you, as well as group therapy. And the ranch optional activities. In addition to what you see there, anyone is free to participate in any of the ranching chores around here. Heaven knows we could use the help, but we do have ranch hands and we can carry on without you if it isn't your thing."

She nodded. "I've never done much ranching, but I think I'd like to see what it's all about, so count me in."

"Excellent." She took a couple steps toward the door. "I'll let you get settled in. Bear is welcome to stay in the house or outside in the barn or garage, like I said. We got Frankie and Casper out there, two of the best cattle dogs you've ever seen, but they're working dogs. He's been so good and quiet, I bet he'd be just fine in here."

Bear sat next to the bed, just watching them. "He's a good boy. Let's see how he does."

Kellie turned to leave.

"But thank you. Sleeping with him helps. He's not quite a therapy dog. Never been trained like that. I just use him that way."

"Believe me. I can understand that." She laughed. "But he is the largest dog I've ever seen and that's for sure."

"He's called a Newfoundland. But I think he's even large for that breed."

"Well, he's a real sweetheart, I'll tell you what."

As soon as Eden was left to herself, she moved to the window. Her view was amazing. With a hand on Bear's head, she tried to take in the property from all visible directions. Woods, greenery, outbuildings, fencing. The place was as picturesque as any she'd seen.

Her phone dinged. Without really planning to, she picked it up.

Hey it's Reid.

She went into partial panic mode. Was he really hurt? Had he called to let her know that his scrapes were infected? As question after question poured into her mind, her breathing became faster and more frantic. With shaking hands, she tried to ignore him, but she knew if she just left it there, the unanswered text would pick at her.

Hello, what can I do for you?

Just letting you know I got a call from Nigel Fensteen on the board of directors. I'm happy to serve on the board but I'm gonna be doing conference calls for the meetings.

That is just fine.

She wished he were present at the meetings, but Zoom would have to do. There were a number of things that required bodies actually in town. But she couldn't very well complain when she'd left town as well.

When will you be back?

Five months.

Wow. What did Reid Browning do that he was going to be out of town for five months? She placed her phone down. It didn't matter. She was going to live her life and be happy, no matter what he did with his.

And when she went back to Virginia in a month, happily, she would not run into him.

Chapter 5

Reid waited for her to say more in response to their texting conversation. He had things to do, but he stood there, staring at his phone in case she texted back.

Welcome aboard. Thank you for serving. I appreciate all your father does in this industry.

Something. Anything. But she had stopped sending texts. Fine. Not even a question about how he was feeling after their fall. Which was not great.

His entire back ached deep in the muscles and hurt skin level, too. He'd scraped up his shoulder and back pretty bad. His arms ached from pull-ups; his skin felt like it was on fire. He'd had to sit next to an equally broad man on the plane who kept bumping him, shooting knives across his skin. He didn't know what he was gonna do about the injuries.

Bareback.

He was obviously going to be in intense pain when he got back on a horse. It would hurt to hold on. His skin would rub against his clothes. But he was here to win, and everyone knew that the bareback riders were no strangers to pain. Everything about the event hurt. What were a few more scrapes? He winced as his back stuck to his shirt when he moved.

He reached for the ibuprofen and downed three more pills. That might take the edge off.

Then he stepped outside, squinted his eyes against the welcoming Texas sun, and breathed deeply. The animals, the blue sky, the horizon that stretched in every direction. He was home. And despite all the pain and irritation, having to be with his dad the past week, the event, and the get-under-a-man's-skin-annoying Eden Cooper, he was back. And he was about to get up on a horse. Suddenly a grin filled his face.

"José!"

"Hey, look who's home." The man peeked around the corner of the barn as Reid strode toward it.

"It couldn't happen any sooner. How early can we get me up on a bareback?"

"As soon as two minutes." José's eyes sharpened. "But why are you walking crooked?" He stepped closer and circled around Reid. "And you're standing lopsided." He stepped closer. "And you're all scraped up? Wow, what did you fight while you were gone? And how come he won?"

She. Eden's face came to mind immediately, but he pushed it aside.

"It's nothing. You've seen me in worse scrapes."

"Maybe. You sure you want to ride today? This looks fresh."

"I want to ride, right now, or I'm gonna lose my mind."

José held up his hands. "Okay, boss. Say no more." He called into the barn. "Get Spitfire ready. Reid is going up."

The sounds of a busy barn made Reid happy. The

neighing of horses, their nickering, the hoses, spraying things down, the smells. He walked to the fence, staring out across the soft sand in the arena. Getting the Original Six together again had been a good call. He'd have to thank Ryan when he saw him later. The guys were cooking meat at the ranch tonight. One more thing that had been off these last couple weeks was shifting more to the right. The guys. He pulled out his phone and snapped a selfie, sending it off to The Chute. "I'm baaaaack and bringing steaks."

All the funny gagging emojis about his selfie made him laugh. "Hey, cut the crap. I'm getting on Spitfire in about thirty seconds. I've got my life in my hands…"

"Cry me a river." Westin, who rode bulls, sent a GIF of some crazed blonde crying hysterically.

He shook his head and set the phone on the fence rail. "José!"

"We're ready for you." He waved from the far chute.

Reid jogged over, every piece of him complaining. But he ignored it all. He had to get back up.

José was working as chute boss today.

Reid lowered himself onto Spitfire, one hand gripping the rope and the other holding onto the metal rail. He held his legs out in front of him and got ready to find that balance.

"Spitfire is mad this morning. Apparently he doesn't like Mondays." José winked.

"Eight seconds."

"You got this. It takes you longer than eight seconds to put on your boots."

He nodded. "Go."

José cinched Spitfire, making him truly want to spit fire, if his lunge out of the chute was any indication, and Reid forgot all about the pain.

People talked about eight seconds being quick. "You can do anything for eight seconds." He heard it all the time. But in the moment of the ride, eight seconds might as well be an hour. Each one dragged along in milliseconds, every movement cataloged and analyzed a hundred ways, until the buzzer sounded and he leapt from the animal. Today was no different. But somewhere around second four, a sort of realization hit him: that he was getting bucked around on the back of a horse that he couldn't touch with his legs, could only hold on with one hand while it did crazy gymnastics beneath him, and he was loving every minute of it. He started to laugh and then shouted, "Wooohooo!" through his teeth. Only an idiot would open his mouth while riding bareback.

The buzzer rang out after eight seconds, and he leapt off. Spitfire was still going at it. Another four or five seconds more until he got out all his fire. They uncinched him and he trotted back to the exit. All in a day's work for that animal. Reid went back to José. "That went well."

"Except for you calling out like some weird prairie coyote, I think the judges would have scored that high. Welcome back." He held out a fist to tap.

"Let's do it again."

José looked like he would complain, but Reid hopped up on the chute. "With Devil's Spawn."

"You got some kind of death wish? Tell me now. There are easier ways to go."

"Nah, I gotta get this back in my blood. That felt too new."

"Looked good to me…"

Reid held up a finger and circled it in the air. "One more round."

José hopped down and called in, "Devil's Spawn's up."

When their head trainer and stable hand returned to join him up on the metal railings, Reid grinned.

"You're a crazy man."

"Maybe I am. But this is where I'm happiest. You can't begrudge a man his happiness."

"Did you get that land you were after?"

Reid nodded. "I sure did. Acres of it between here and San Antonio, and then more on the other side as well."

"Whatcha gonna do with all that cactus?"

He winked. "Oh, there's more than cactus. Besides, the jelly ain't half bad."

"My mama taught me right. Prickly pear nothing is entering this belly."

"I bet Kellie could change your mind. That's the first place I had some."

He didn't look convinced.

"You coming to the meat fest tonight?"

"I got my own set of plans. But next time."

"Oh? And what are these plans?"

They led Devil's Spawn to the chute. Reid could see the fire in his eyes. "Wow, I think you're right. None of these guys likes a good ride on Monday morning." He shook his head. "As if they're doing any of the work."

"You hear that, Devil's Spawn, this mug here thinks you're a lazy lightweight who can't pull his weight."

The horse grunted and his flank quivered.

"That'll get him." José shifted his position.

Reid lowered himself again, gripping the ropes, holding onto the metal rails. "Eight seconds."

"Yeah, we know, we know." He cinched the horse.

Reid could feel the energy beneath him. "Go."

Devil's Spawn tore out through the opened gate. And

the minute his feet hit the sand, he jumped all four in the air, twisting mid-jump, and dumped Reid in the dirt.

José and the other hands tore out, pushing him back before he brought hooves down on Reid's head.

He jumped up. "Do it again."

"Again?"

"Yup. Same horse."

José shook his head, but Reid ran for the chute. "Hurry while he's still angry."

A hesitant José brought a kicking, fuming horse back into the chute.

Reid lowered himself on and they tore out again. This time, Reid was determined not to drop until the horse gave up. The buzzer rang, but he held on. José's voice in the background called to him, but he tuned the man out. Devil's Spawn leapt and bucked and turned and might have even tried to nip him in the leg, but Reid held on. He had no idea how much time passed. It could have been an afternoon for all it felt like to him, but at last the horse slowed. He rested. Bucked one more time and then walked back to the entrance.

Reid jumped off.

"You trying to train the horse to stop bucking?" José, looking more than furious, grabbed the reins, uncinched the horse and stomped back toward the barn, shouting, "Someone brush down Devil's Spawn."

Reid knew what he was doing. Sometimes the rider needed a little training as well as the horse. He was sure that guy would be plenty mad next go-round.

And Reid would be ready for him. "I'm taking a shower."

José's grumbling didn't even translate into anything

intelligible at this point. Reid was back. He had his game, and he was going to win the contest tomorrow.

Chapter 6

Eden woke up to a docket full of work. The minute she left town everyone needed her for something, it seemed like. But as she started to go through emails one at a time, she forgot where she was and the typical worries of a typical workday descended.

Bear whined.

"Oh hey, boy. Wanna go outside?"

He leapt up and then nudged her with his nose.

She closed her laptop, determined not to let work take over. She'd felt she needed this time away. Time to make the most of the quiet, of everything that was different here than what she was used to out in Arlington.

Her first meeting wasn't for another couple hours, so she followed Bear outside. They exited onto the back porch, and Eden smiled in pleased surprise. The porch ran the width of the house, wide and painted crisp and new. Hammock chairs hung from the ceiling.

Another woman, a short and curvy redhead, waved

from the opposite end. She climbed into one of the chairs with a book. "You new?"

"Just got here. I'm Eden."

"Tracey. You're gonna love it. I've been here a week and never want to leave."

"That's great to hear."

"I don't want to stop your exploring. This place is amazing. I'm sure I'll see you at group chat later this afternoon."

"Right. Okay." She waved and then followed the not so patient Bear out into the back yard.

"Go, Bear! Run!"

He didn't wait for another command, but took off toward the back of the property.

She laughed, watching him go. He must have been holding in all the smells, resisting the temptation to run after them, this whole time. What a good dog.

Horses ran in a group behind the white fence to her right. With manes in the breeze and tails high and flowing out behind them, they were a stunning sight. She headed toward them.

They circled out toward the other side of the pasture until someone whistled. She turned her head all around, but saw no one near. But the horses turned in one mass and came running to the fence.

For a minute, she thought they were going to jump the fence and run her over, but they stopped a short distance from her. A few nickered.

She'd not been around horses ever, just always admired them. "Hey there, guys." She held out a hand.

But they pretty much ignored her. She laughed. "I see how this works." She reached down for a handful of grass and held it out.

Then three headed toward her, bumping one another to arrive first.

She held her hand out, palm flat and up, and a beautiful speckled grey and white horse took it from her. She ripped up some more, feeding all three until the others joined and wanted some also.

Laughing, she pet their noses and sides and gave them as much grass as they wanted.

The ranch, she discovered, was full of moments like these. The barn had pigs and a mama who was giving birth to piglets. The other back pasture had cows. There were goats in pens and plenty of birds everywhere. Bear was in heaven, chasing every living thing he could find in range of his huge paws and nose.

Her feet took her to a huge barn, the only place in walking distance she hadn't explored yet. Then her phone dinged. Time for the first appointment with Kellie. She looked back at the house. Wow, she'd come a long way. The barn doors opened and a tall man stepped out. "Hey. You new today?"

"I am. I'm Eden. I just realized I'm supposed to be up at the house in five minutes." She eyed the four wheelers that were parked behind him.

"Oh sure, you want to take one of these out? They're available to all the guests. Sign one out here and you can keep it all week if you like, or two weeks. How long are you staying?"

"I'm here for three." Was that long? Had she signed up for too long?

"Oh, that's even better." He handed her a clipboard and pen. She wrote her name.

He took it back and hung it on a nearby wall. "I'm Ryan. Kellie is my sister."

"Oh, she told me you'd be around." Her smile grew naturally across her mouth. "Thanks for the four-wheeler."

"No problem. The key is in the ignition. Should start up like a champ."

She started it and then slowly pulled past Ryan. "Thanks again."

He waved, friendly, reminding her that she missed genuine human friendliness and hospitality. It was a gift and important. She could be more…friendly. So often she was in a hurry, pushing through the drive-thru for dinner, rushing through the lines at the store. Who did she interact with? And how much of a difference was she making in their lives? Before a round of guilt could descend, she reminded herself that of course she was making a difference. Vets 4 Life was one of the most important things happening on the Hill as far as she was concerned. And raising awareness of her issues and seeking opportunities to help assist vets was a passion. But…she could be more like this Ryan. And stop and smile now and then.

The four-wheeler was strangely freeing and she decided to take it out every day. Bear came bounding up, barking as he ran alongside. "Hey, boy!" She laughed.

When she pulled up to the house, she left the key in the ignition like she'd found it and told Bear to stay outside.

The house smelled like someone had melted caramel all over a brownie. And her stomach grumbled.

The table was spread with lunch.

"Oh wow."

"Kellie always has the best spread. And it's great for every diet." The voice behind her sounded warm. Its owner looked warm. A curvy woman, older than Eden by a few years or by some life experience, and with a ready smile.

"There's too much of it." Another voice from around

the corner joined them as they entered the dining room. The woman she'd met on the porch, Tracey, smiled back at her. Her hair had been pulled up on her head, most of the curls contained. Another woman joined through the opposite door. Her deep brown skin, her hair long and in corn rows, and hanging down her shoulders, her eyes deep and brown. It was like looking at a model, her features perfect. For a moment Eden was mesmerized. Then she blinked. "Hey."

They joined her at the table. Two more sat with them and then Kellie entered. "Hello. Let's get the food served. We can start eating and then we'll get to it."

Eden added soup to her bowl. And a corn muffin. She filled her water cup. Everything smelled so good.

Kellie lifted her spoon. "Two new guests today. Eden Cooper." She indicated further down the table. "And Mary Hortez." A closed, perhaps even sullen looking, woman looked down at her lap. "Let's start by hearing from you two. If you could introduce yourselves."

Kellie looked at Eden first, so she scrambled to think of the best way to present herself here. "I'm, um. Eden, as she said. I live in Virginia outside Washington, DC."

"I'm Mary." She closed her mouth and looked down at her food. Apparently, that was all they were going to hear from Mary.

The food tasted as good as it smelled and when it was finally cleared away, Eden felt more comfortable than she had when they began.

"Let's get started." Kellie lifted her paperwork up to the table in front of her. "Everyone has a chance to talk. I think we will start with a more detailed introduction from our two new guests. Perhaps tell us why you are here. And then, you can share whatever you like here. Our job in these sessions is just to listen."

Eden nodded and a nice feeling of freedom filled her. This was a safe place. She'd never see these women again. "I'm here because I…" Her brain scrambled. She lost the word she was about to say, everything that she had been thinking a moment before left, and she forgot the question. "Sorry. This happens. I just forgot everything I was about to say." Her hands shook.

"Don't worry hon, happens to the best of us." Tracey's face was encouraging.

But Eden couldn't get the right words to form. "I'd like to get myself back. I want this, memory thing to stop. I want…to feel at peace again." She shook her head, surprised at her outburst.

Kellie looked like she wanted to hug Eden, but her warm eyes just smiled back and then she looked down the table at Mary.

"I'm here because they're making me show improvement before I can get my son back." Mary frowned.

"Welcome to you. We are all about connection here. Improvement is entirely up to you." Kellie turned to the others. "Why don't you all take a turn and then we'll focus on our work for the day."

As Eden listened to the stories of each of the other guests, she was in turns astonished at the causes of their broken hearts, admiring of the wisdom they had learned while here at the ranch and also, lonely. She really didn't belong with them. They had been left, broken, beaten down, and she…she had neurological damage from explosions while serving in Iraq. A small voice inside whispered of her own injured heart, but she brushed it aside as unrelated, not applicable, and entirely not a big deal.

"We're going dancing tonight." Kellie put both hands on the table. "And I know a great group of guys here for the rodeo, friends of Ryan's if you're nervous about men. These six know we're not looking for anything romantic. But they're available to have some fun."

Eden nodded. That was nice, a no expectations opportunity for a fun night. "What time do we leave?"

"Nine o'clock on the dot."

She suspected here in Lost Creek she would find decent, well-mannered, men. And if she was lucky, they just might be respectful on top of it all. And after the people she surrounded herself with day in and out, the thought of changing up her crowd appealed almost as much as anything else on this ranch.

Chapter 7

Reid showed up at the ranch that night through the back gate entrance. His truck sped along the old dirt road, like no one else used it, because they didn't. Or if they did, you could see their dust coming for miles. The sun set late on these early spring days and he was enjoying the warm night, the soft glow of the land all around him, and the feel of a truck rumbling over land beneath. How could his dad not want this life?

He shifted his weight. His dad probably asked the same thing about Reid not wanting anything to do with a legal career. They were two men as different as he'd ever seen two humans, and yet one had sired the other. His phone dinged. A quick glance at the screen resting on the seat at his side told him that the purchase of his land had gone through officially.

A deep satisfaction settled in around him. His own land. It was currently home to a whole herd of Longhorns. He'd purchased them as well, to keep the agricultural use up and his taxes appropriate. In a couple weeks the surveyors would be out and the location for his homestead would be plotted.

He was itching to go take a look. It wasn't far from Ryan's. An hour, maybe two. He grinned. When in Texas, the miles spread out and the time did too. Maybe he could slip away later this week.

A tumble of dust moved along the road toward him. It was still plenty far, but Reid was curious about who it could be. The ranch was home to as many as ten women at a time, but from what he'd heard, the ladies spent most of their time up at the house, or closer to the barns helping out. While his gaze was glued to the rising dust cloud, his truck swerved about on the road. He focused again on where he was driving when a huge black creature bounded out to cross the road in front of him. He slammed on the brakes and swerved, cursing himself for doing it, as the truck skid, the tires locked, and he went sliding off the dirt road across the rocks and prickly pear that filled the property on all sides. He had new tires. Should be fine.

He heard no thump, so he probably missed the creature. But he winced, thinking about it as the truck came to a stop. Dust billowed up all around him. He craned his neck in all directions, but couldn't see head or tail of anything that resembled that blurred massive dark thing in his path. He let his breathing settle a minute, and then he turned the key to start the truck and get going. Nothing. "Nah, come on. You're tougher than this. It's a little dirt." He tried again. Nothing, not even a click. He got out, his boots stepping on a prickly pear, closed his door, and moved around to the hood.

He'd forgotten about the incoming dust cloud until the sound of tires on dirt road hit him. As he lifted the hood, he half kept an eye for someone showing up, filling his lungs with some more dust.

And now that his truck wouldn't start, a ride to the house would be nice.

The engine looked fine. He wasn't an expert, but nothing he'd expected to be shaken free was. It didn't feel especially overheated either.

The incoming vehicle turned out to be a four-wheeler. A wind blew some of the dust cloud away and he easily made out a lone figure, heading toward him on the road.

He closed the hood and moved back around to the driver's seat. But turning the key still did nothing. He wasn't sure why he thought staring at the engine would have made a difference, but sometimes the passage of time did. He shrugged, then slid back out and stood on the road as the four-wheeler drew nearer.

A woman.

She pulled to a stop, inviting another dust cloud, then slipped off her ATV. Her back was to him as she brought hands up to her face. A loud whistle pierced the air around them. "Bear."

A bark, and then the large dark creature he'd almost hit, who'd caused this whole mess, came barreling toward her. Reid could only stare. What was that thing? "Hey!" He waved.

She turned.

His mouth dropped. "Eden?" He had no words, nothing to help him understand her presence on this land.

"Wha—?" Then she shook her head, her words apparently stuck in her throat, a look of alarm taking over her face.

"Bear!"

Two paws barreled into his chest, throwing him off

balance. He stumbled back, his boot catching on something the sent him flat on his back.

Something sharp shook his brain in a way he'd never experienced, like maybe things rattled inside. Then the world went black.

He woke up to Ryan's voice, and Lars? Then a woman he didn't know. While the grogginess began to clear, he kept his eyes closed. No sound of Eden. He had to have imagined that woman standing here on the ranch. There was no way Eden was here. Was he losing it? And the dog? But how had he fallen? What happened to him, and where was he now? He shifted his fingers. Not in the dirt. Maybe a bed?

"I know you're listening." *Eric*. Classic.

"I can't hear a word you're saying." The words he thought he said came out garbled and unintelligible. His eyes flew open. But the world was blurry. "What's happening to me?" Again, unintelligible words sounded in his ears.

The others' voices were quiet. He could only see a woman he didn't know, blonde, almost the same hair color as Eden. He closed his eyes, relieved. He must have seen this new woman and imagined Eden.

A hand rested on his shoulder, not a woman's hand. "Stay with us ya drama queen."

"He always did want all the attention." Definitely Westin. Bull rider. Typical.

Reid tried talking again. Something simple. "Ha." It worked.

"You with us?" Ford's face peered over Reid's.

Reid tried to nod, but pain shot to his shoulder. "Ouch."

"Yep. He's with us now. You'd think he just rode bareback by the way he's carrying on." Eric's smile was always obvious in his voice.

"Unlike some people who just ride bulls." That came out mushy until the word bulls.

The guys laughed. "Yep, talking smack about bull riders. He's back."

"All right. Keep him talking until the doctor gets here."

"Paying a house call?"

"Dr. Mills was on his way home, said he'd stop by, and that it might be better not to move him anyway."

"The question I have is, did he bring the steaks?" Eric again.

Reid tried to snort, but it came out as more of a strangled cough and the room grew quiet.

"In the truck." That was more clear.

"Well at least we have the steaks."

They were trying for humor, but Reid could tell he had them scared. He had himself scared. What no one knew was that he was doing his best just to hold things together. Trying to speak, but things coming out garbled? Had he had a stroke? Was his face paralyzed? He tried moving his lips and wrinkling his nose.

"Whatcha doing there, Reid?" Ford.

"I can move my face." Would they understand?

"Ah, thinks he's paralyzed. Let's check it out." Eric's face appeared above him. "Move your foot."

Reid ignored him mostly and went through every body part. Then he nodded. "I'm good."

"Okay, doctor's here. All the rest of you get that meat going or we're never gonna make it to the bar dance place by nine." The woman with the blonde hair maybe, was speaking.

"Yes, ma'am."

The room felt vast and lonely when they'd all left. And cold. His limbs started to tremble. And he couldn't make them stop.

But a blanket soon covered him to his chin, and he started to calm.

An older gentleman's kindly eyes peered down at him. "Now what happened here?" He shone a light in Reid's eyes. "Did anyone see it?"

"Yes, this young lady here."

Reid couldn't see anything but what was right in his line of sight, and he didn't like moving his head because it hurt and he was afraid of shaking it up worse. But he heard a voice, muffled and quiet, but familiar. And he began to doubt his memory. Why would she be here? It just couldn't be Eden Cooper. He was losing it.

"Big dog."

"What was that, Reid? Sounds like you are getting your voice back." The doctor lifted his hand, moved his fingers around, and then investigated his legs and feet, rotating them in full circles.

"Big dog."

"Ah yes. I heard you were knocked to the ground by Bear. I can totally understand. I met that animal coming in and I've never seen a larger dog." He clucked his tongue while he continued poking and prodding Reid and all his joints.

Then he moved to his head. "Let's lift you." He carefully lifted Reid's head and rotated it from one side to the other. "They said you helped them and walked in, holding your neck upright. I'm not worried about any broken bones at least."

Had he? He had no memory of anything after landing on his back.

"Are you having pain right now?"

"Yes."

"More when I move your head?"

Reid considered. "No, when I move it."

"Ah, so supporting your head and moving slowly is not causing pain."

He tried to nod and then groaned.

"But your nodding seems to have hurt."

"Yes."

After several more minutes of the doctor doing things and moving things and making thinking noises, he peered over the bed again and looked into Reid's eyes. "Nothing serious, I don't think. You might be concussed. And since you're in so much pain, I recommend lying still for a couple days and then taking it easy for two weeks. Go get yourself a scan too, just to see what's happened inside."

"Rodeo?"

"Oh no. Give it a full two weeks before you're back up on a horse. Then take it easy. Pay attention to your head. If it feels rattled or painful, take it easy."

He groaned.

"Be patient. I'm assuming you're gonna want your head around for a few more years?"

He started to nod and then sucked in his breath. "Yes."

"I'm writing a prescription for pain medication. Without a narcotic, given that you are here in this home with these women. You won't have to move so much. If you need something stronger, give me a call."

"Thank you." He resisted most pain meds except for ibuprofin, but he was gonna need something. Lying here, staring at the ceiling was not going to cut it.

"You are welcome. Now I hope you get better soon. You

couldn't have fallen into a more capable caretaker than our Kellie here."

"Mm."

"I'll give you a call tomorrow to check up on you."

The doctor left the room, and his voice and other women's continued down the hall. He closed his eyes. He was seeing Eden Cooper out on the dirt roads of the ranch. He hadn't told the doctor he was seeing things. But if it happened again, he'd need to maybe see the psychiatrist boss had been hinting about.

Chapter 8

Eden hadn't told anyone she knew Reid. She was still trying to grapple with all of it herself.

Tammy stared open mouthed after hearing the details of what happened. "Bear knocked him flat?" All the women gathered round her in the front room, the opposite side of the house where Reid lay. And Eden stood and began pacing. "How was I to know he was gonna knock the man down? He had almost run Bear over a few moments before…"

"What! What kind of man would run down your dog?" Mary frowned deeper than usual.

She waved her hands. "No. I'm sure he's a perfectly great man. Bear leapt out in front of his truck. I just don't know what to do about any of this." She wrung her hands together. "Do you think he will be okay?"

"I think so. I bet it's just a concussion."

Those words jarred. *Just a concussion.* She had a concussion. Her concussion is what changed her life and made her daily existence that much more difficult. It was her concussion that the doctors would never be able to cure, they said. The results of her concussion were the reason she'd come in the first place. But she didn't respond, just sat back down.

And what on earth was Reid Browning doing out here in the middle of nowhere Texas at the Broken Hearts Ranch?

"What did you say he does here?" She turned to Kellie who had joined them.

"He's an icon around here, one of the Original Six."

When no one seemed to know what she was talking about, she laughed. "To us, that's as good as any football team." She sat with them. "They started at our Sam Houston Community College, just outside of town, maybe forty minutes from here and created the first rodeo team. They were good, dang good. And by the time they left, had quite a following. And plenty of wins and sponsors besides. Ryan, my brother, was a part of all that. An injury forced him to quit, but the others have kept at it and some of them headed for national tours. They're good, every last one of them. And the nicest guys. They're the ones coming to dance tonight. Well, all except Reid I'd imagine. Which is a right shame."

When the other women laughed and started talking about how handsome he was, Kellie shook her head. "I'm not talking about the way the man looks. Heaven knows he's something to look at. No. He's a tall glass, that one, and full of manners and the right amount of distance. He's nothing but pure cowboy respect, I tell you."

Eden couldn't believe any of this woman's words. She knew they must be true, but the Reid she knew, or thought she knew, was a fast-talking lawyer with little care for anything but himself. Right? She shook her head. And he'd entertained six women that night, left with two on his arms. He'd been so...difficult. Had she rubbed him so wrong that all she saw was his difficult side?

That couldn't be. Eden prided herself on her ability to read people. But what did she know? After seeing Reid here...

And she'd hurt him. Again. Her head dropped forward into her hands.

"Oh, come on honey, he's gonna be all right." Tracey rested a hand on her shoulder.

She nodded, but she wasn't so sure. She knew about concussions and the long-lasting effects they could have on a person. "Just a concussion" was not something anyone should say.

"Should we get out the games? Our evening's been a little bit disorganized with our new guest, but let's play some Scrabble, hearts, checkers, whatever you can find in those drawers, before we go get ready for some dancing!" She grinned.

Tracey, who had been here longer, sifted through the games and soon they were all involved in something, but Eden was only half present. She knew it might be a long time before she began to understand the range of emotions rushing through her like a torrent. But the other ladies had moved on in conversation and Eden was left to nurse her thoughts alone.

When it came time to go dancing, Eden felt a bit better, like maybe she could enjoy herself without an overwhelming weight of guilt.

They climbed into two trucks. Ryan drove one and Kellie the other. Eden climbed in the front next to Kellie, who was full of energy. She wore what Eden would describe as a cowgirl shirt. It was pink with fringe hanging across the front and down her arms.

Would the others wear something similar? The locals? The ladies at the house all dressed more like Eden did. She wore a black skirt, white blouse. The outfit was simple but accentuated her curves just enough, and she could move in it. Perfect.

As they pulled up, she could hear the bass thumping out to the street from inside the large wooden building. The parking lot was full.

"This is gonna be a fun one. The whole county showed up." Kellie laughed. "Come on!"

The energy was high, even in Mary who had been so sullen before. Looked like a little fun on the dance floor was a universal stress relief. And boy could Eden use it. She let a long breath leave her slowly and with it most of her worries. Kellie stepped up beside her. She had told the woman about her aversion to most men she knew. When Kellie had asked about the military leaders, from her squadron leader to her general, Eden considered each one and wondered if she'd just reached her fill of men in authority. She hadn't had time to consider where her thoughts would take her when pursuing that direction. So much had happened. At the center of her distraction was, of course, the arrival of Reid. Reid. The kind of guy she could see in most positions of authority she'd known in her life; all about being right, being in charge and all about attention. It was like they fueled their life on the accolades of others, the fawning women, or subduing others. But then she'd seen other sides to him… she pushed those thoughts aside. She'd just focus on making sure he recovered and then never see him again, if possible. Certainly, she needed to stop injuring him.

Kellie was studying her face. Eden could only guess

what she was about to say. "These men are just here for a bit of fun. None of them is trying to prove anything and tonight is all about letting go of all that stuff that's making you frown."

She laughed at her boldness. "You, Kellie, are trying to create trouble."

"Only the good kind."

They linked arms, almost like old friends might, and Eden thought it nice. It had been many years since she'd felt the simple friendship that Kellie seemed to offer. They opened the door to loud music and the smell of french fries and beer.

Kellie waved and when Eden turned to see who their company would be, she clutched Kellie's arm. "Are they for real?"

"Every one of them. Reid too. But you know where he is." Her face looked innocent enough. It certainly wasn't like Kellie to rub in Eden's discomfort.

Four tall, broad cowboys approached. And Eden's palms started to sweat for the first time in forever. The other women from the house crowded in close to Kellie so that Eden was pushed more to the back. Which was fine by her. She needed to catch her breath and her wits. They were just a bunch of guys. Model looking strong cowboys, but just guys.

They laughed together, the women introducing themselves, the guys probably telling their names, but Eden couldn't hear any of it over the music. Kellie pointed at Eden who waved and smiled. Then the music turned slow and the guys started pairing off. The man named Lars asked Kellie, and Eden watched her walk away as if a lifeline were leaving her behind. Just when Eden thought she might sit this one out, the strong wiry one held out a hand. "I'm Westin. Would you like to dance?"

"Sure." She tried to act like this wasn't a high school dance even though that's exactly how she felt. He led her out towards his friends. And then pulled her close, not too close, but nice, friendly close. He held out one hand to their sides and he started slow, rocking back and forth. "So, Eden Cooper. Where are you from?"

They shared the basic information everyone learns.

"So, you six are the original guys to start rodeo in this town?"

"More or less. It existed before us, of course. But we started it at the community college and the town seemed to go crazy." He shrugged. "Reid is the one you need to talk to about that whole thing."

"Reid?" She was intrigued in spite of herself.

"Oh yeah. He's the reason the town loved it so much, with his homegrown cowboy congeniality." He watched her, as if waiting for her to agree with him.

She didn't know what to say. "I guess I don't know him well enough."

"Yep. He's our chute boss too, which stands for something around here."

"Chute boss?"

"Well, I guess technically we hope that's gonna be Ryan's job. But we call Reid the chute boss too, 'cause he's always taking care of things. He's telling us all what to do and where to do it. But in a good way, you know?" He spun her around. And she hardly noticed, so distracted by the different version of Reid his best friends told. Westin was strong. Her hand on his shoulder felt only muscle rotating beneath her fingers. He spun her again. "So how are you liking the ranch?"

"I've only been there for a day, but I think it is going to be good for me." She surprised herself at even that small reveal to a relative stranger.

"Kellie is one in a million. There's nothing me and the guys wouldn't do for her."

"She's lucky to have you guys." They sounded so much like a family. A twinge of envy led her to wish to spend more time with any of them.

Westin led her to the tall, dark and beautiful Ford. She lifted her chin higher to see him. "How are you liking the most happening place in Lost Creek?"

"You joke, but this is better than anything I do at home."

Ford's ready smile warmed her further.

He tipped his head. "And what are you smiling about?"

"You. You're so friendly."

"Well now, I think any man in this room is gonna be friendly to a pretty lady in a dance hall." He tipped his hat and winked at her.

"You would be surprised. So often you know exactly why a man is being friendly. And that's different."

"And how do you know I'm not just like all of them?"

She studied him for a moment. How did she know? "I don't know. It's a hunch, and Kellie vouched for all of you and I trust that woman."

"As you should. And you're correct in your thinking. We're harmless, some more than others."

She thought of Reid and his attention to the other ladies and her earlier impressions of him. So he would likely be one of the more arrogant ones.

"We're all scoundrels in one way or another. The only one of us you could rely on all the time is Reid."

"Reid?" She tried to hide her shock, but it must have been clear as day on her face.

"Do you know Reid?"

"Um." She didn't know how to answer that. Yes, she knew Reid, or so she thought. She'd been caught by Reid as they skid across the gravel paths at the Mall in Washington, DC. Reid worked on the board of her non-profit. Reid had almost run over her dog and then been knocked to the ground by him. "I don't think I know him well at all."

"He's gonna be laid up for a while and the man could use a bit of a distraction. It's gonna drive him crazy not to be moving, and I don't even know what he'll do when he can't be up on his horse."

"How long does he have to be in bed?"

"I don't know, but he can't ride for at least two weeks and I think that right there might strike the man dead."

Their music ended. Ford grinned. "Thank you for the dance. Tell me more about your job."

"I work to help war veterans, especially ones with neurological damage. And I have a think tank, a lobbying firm out in Washington, DC." Most people didn't know much at all about anything she did. The world of lobbying and even non-profits felt foreign to them.

"Can you make any money doing that?"

She laughed. "Enough, I guess. I'm not really doing it for the money. Do you make money doing rodeo?"

"If I do it right." His bold charm set her at ease.

"When can I see you guys in a rodeo?"

"This weekend. We're right here in Lost Creek, which is another reason why Reid is gonna go crazy. You have to help that guy."

"What could I do?"

"I don't know. Nurse him back to health. Make him stay still. You seem the most likely to be able to do anything."

"What? Me?"

"Well, yeah. Now I mean this in the most platonic way possible. I hear neither of you is looking for any kind of relationship. So this is perfect. What I mean is, you're his type."

Some new pleasure rolled through her like baseball fans doing the wave. And she was powerless in its wake and mushy and hopeful for more. She cleared her throat. Twice. "Uh."

He shrugged. "I didn't mean to intrude. If you're too busy, I can ask one of the other women as well."

"No." Her answer was more abrupt than she wanted. "I —" What was she about to say? "I'll step in and see what I can do."

"That's what I like to hear. When a cowboy is laid up, the only solace is a woman." He nodded.

"Whatever. Ford. I think you're messing with me a little bit."

"I might be, a little bit, but the truth is, I care a lot about Reid. He's a great guy, and I know this is gonna hit him hard. So. Thank you."

After this dance, their group all climbed into a booth with a table pulled up next to fit them all. She was wedged between two broad shouldered, solid men. Lars, the man on her right had Kellie on his other side and Eden knew right away that his attention was there. Even with his eyes on Eden, he paid attention to her every movement. *Interesting.* Kellie seemed unaware she had an audience in Lars.

Eric sat on her other side. "So, Eden. I understand we have you to thank for a tour in Iraq."

Everyone paused and turned to her. But their expressions were open and curious, friendly, and respectful.

"Does Reid know that?" Westin downed a couple gulps of water.

"I—" Baffled about why that would matter at all, she struggled to know what to say.

"It might make it easier on him that her dog ran him over." Ryan laughed and shared some kind of humor with the other guys.

Eric held both hands out. "Whoa, hold on. There's a couple things we gotta unpack here. One. I really do want to hear about Iraq. And two....your dog?"

Ryan's eyes twinkled with amusement. "It's more of a... wolf creature."

Attention shifted back to her.

"Well, if Reid hadn't almost run Bear over, he might not have been so keen on putting paws on the man's chest."

"So, this huge creature he keeps talking about? That's your dog?" Eric's eyes widened and everyone seemed more amused than they should be.

"I feel terrible about it. But yes. Bear is mine." She fiddled with her napkins. Did she tell them also that she and Reid knew each other? She saw no need. They didn't really know each other, anyway. "Do you think he'll be okay?"

"With lots of women waiting on him hand and foot?" Westin snorted. "The man will be fine."

"If he doesn't sneak out and ride bare first." Eric pointed a fork in Westin's direction.

"Right. But I got Eden on that. She's gonna keep him in bed and happy." Ford winked and Eden was about to refute her duty when Tracey piped up. The other women had been quiet, watching the men center all attention on Eden, talking with each other. Except Kellie who laughed openly like these guys were brothers. Eden would like that. These men as family. She smiled.

"And see, she's happy about it." Eric jabbed her.

But Tracey sat forward. "I could keep him in bed." She smiled and Eden almost choked on her water. Had she meant what she said? Or was her naïve expression real? The guys shifted around uncomfortably until Ford said, "You do that. He will need a guard or two at the door, keeping him in place."

She nodded and then wiggled back in her seat, overly pleased.

"I'll help too," Eden surprised herself by adding. "I feel responsible actually. I'll keep him off his feet and off his horse, until he's healed." She wanted to add that if he had a concussion he never would fully heal.

Ford seemed satisfied and then Eric leaned back. "Now on to my first question. Iraq. Thank you."

Something about his *thank you*. Simple. Two words. It touched her. And she found herself wanting to tear up. She returned his gaze. "You are welcome." And he was. There were some Americans who would make the problems worse and she might have said you're welcome to them too, but when she said it to Eric, it was one of those experiences where she knew she might even do it again, if asked. For guys like him. These were Reid's friends? And they cared so much about him. He certainly surrounded himself with good people. She could see that with friends like these, he wouldn't want to spend more time in Washington, DC, at least not with the people she was accustomed to out there. Maybe they had more in common in that regard than she realized.

Too much to really think about for one day crowded her mind. This trip to Texas was more enlightening than she'd predicted. And in ways she'd least expected. But she was willing to see to Reid. Her conscience would feel better if he recovered. And she could certainly put him in contact with the right people to talk to about his concussion.

She thought about her new assignment from the guys for the rest of the evening. And she thought about their opinion of Reid. The more she wondered, the less sure she felt about any of her previous assessments of the man.

Chapter 9

Reid thought he was going die.

One after another of the women in Kellie's house stopped by throughout the day with things they thought might distract him. Maybe that's what they were doing. He had magazines. Crosswords. Sudoku. He liked Sudoku, at least. What he wanted was to get back to his trailer and on his horse.

But he still had twelve days left. Twelve days of women like Tracey, who planted herself in his room at all hours of the day. Sometimes chattering away, sometimes saying nothing, but always these large soulful and…inviting eyes, watching him. And no Eden. She had yet to step foot in his room.

He shook his head.

Tracey moved to his side. "What is it? Would you like some water?"

"No, I'm fine. I think I'll take a nap." He waited and she didn't move.

"Alone? Maybe you could close the door on your way out?"

"Oh! Of course. You sure you don't want company while you sleep?"

"Yep, I'm sure."

As soon as his door closed, he breathed out in relief and then he sat up in bed. He couldn't do this one more day. His head pounded from the movement, but he eased his feet down to the floor and made his way across the room to his boots. Too bad he didn't have something simpler to slip on.

He winced through the motions of pulling on boots, but held his head steady after the jarring, pinpricks of pain that shook him and then carefully stood again. Where was his truck? He pocketed the keys and moved to the window that looked out on the front drive. A line of cars out there showed him no truck. No matter. He would find it. He scanned the area and his eyes fell on the ATV. Yep. That was gonna be his.

Just those simple movements told him he wasn't getting back up on a horse today, but he could rest anywhere, and he'd much rather set up in front of a fire at the fairgrounds than be hounded day and night by well-meaning people. He crept to the door, feeling silly he'd have to sneak, but he didn't really want to answer to Kellie, either.

The door cracked open at his touch, with no loud squeaks to give him away. His boots made noise as they hit the floor, but he stepped out into the hall, shutting the door behind him. He turned to take the hall almost at a run. The door to go out front was in sight. But he had to steady himself for a minute with his hand up against the wall before he moved.

Then he closed his eyes, a dizzy spell taking over.

"You sure that's such a good idea?" *Eden.*

He turned and opened his eyes, willing the house to stop spinning around him. "You really are here."

"I think that's pretty painfully obvious by now."

"But I thought for sure I imagined you. And then I hit my head. It's all a blur now." He rubbed his forehead. "You're really here?"

"Yes, I'm afraid so. You look like you might tip over in your boots. How did you even get those on?" She shook her head and then took his arm. "Let's get you back in there."

"No."

"No?" Her eyebrow rose in such a hint of challenge on her beautiful face, he found himself amused.

"I'm not spending another minute in that bed."

"Is there a chair?"

He nodded. Then groaned from the pain that shot through his head and neck. "But." He sighed. "I can't stand it in there. Can we…" He looked around, desperate for somewhere else they could go.

"How about the back porch?"

"Yes, perfect." One step closer to the ATV and his freedom. He just needed a minute to stop this ridiculous spinning.

"The dizzy spells should ease up."

"How did you know I'm dizzy?" The world faded to grey for a minute and then cleared. "It's pretty bad, actually."

"Take it slow." Her voice was a balm, a cool breeze that floated through him.

"No worries. Every abrupt motion is killing my head."

"It gets better."

He considered her. "You been knocked off your feet by the dog before too?"

She laughed. And then her beautiful voice filled the hall, her face lit, and streams of appreciation lit her eyes. "No, I never have."

He couldn't find a single word to say, but he knew his own smile was growing in ridiculous amounts. She was stunning, so much more beautiful than he'd first thought. Her thick hair was pulled back in a ponytail. Her bare neck and natural look were more appealing than anything to him. And she was being nice to him. Her hands on his arm were cool, like that breeze that refreshed all his concerns.

This was all from bonking his head. He told himself to say nothing that he would regret later, which meant he should probably say nothing at all. But his mouth opened and words started falling out, like a waterfall he had no control over. "You should smile more. You're beautiful."

She froze for a moment and then nodded, patting his arm like he was an invalid. "Thank you. Let's get you situated out here on the porch."

He was not giving an old guy vibe, was he? If she brought him a lap quilt, he'd know he was in trouble.

She tried to hold his arm to help him keep his balance or something, and even though he appreciated her touch, he needed to do something to stamp out this whole memory. After a long shuffling walk through the house and out onto the porch, during which he most definitely felt like an old guy, they were sitting in two Adirondack chairs, looking out over the grounds behind the house.

"This place is so peaceful." She leaned back, seeming at perfect rest.

"Tell me."

"Hmm?"

"Tell me what you know about my head. Have you ever had this?" He waved to his head.

"I think you might have a concussion." She shifted in her chair. "I have what's called an explosion caused concussion, and some neurological damage, from my time in Iraq."

"But you're healed, right? This is gonna go away." It sounded more like a plea than the statement he was hoping to make.

"Yes and no." The sigh that followed sounded tired.

"Tell me."

"So everyone is different, of course. But in my case, they aren't sure the extent of the damage. I find new surprises all the time. Lately I've wanted to explore the emotional effects, the hopes and expectations I have, my reactions to people. I think there are some more things to consider in my case. But as far as the physical injury, I don't get dizzy anymore at all. I can run." Her grin turned mischievous.

And he sat up suddenly. Then of course regretted it. "Yes. You can run like no one I've ever seen." Remembering her at the Mall in DC was the most hopeful news he'd considered. "So you're fine. Your full physical activity has returned."

"Absolutely. But I'm careful. There are some things I would never do."

"Like?" He would ride bareback no matter what anyone told him, but he wanted to be prepared for the worst.

"Like I probably would never play professional football."

He waved his hands. "Be serious."

"Do you want to know what *you* shouldn't do?"

"Yeah, sort of." This conversation had turned back to him rather quickly.

"That's up to your doctor. What they told me was that I

need to be careful of any trauma to the head. Any further injury could bring back all the old symptoms and worse. And, of course, each new concussion creates permanent damage."

"Do you think I'll ride rodeo again?" The question, his most vulnerable at the moment, escaped as all the other words had, without any attention to his restraint. He clung to her response as if all his happiness depended on her next words.

"I can't say." Her eyes filled with compassion which he appreciated. "Right away, I think you can tell it would be better to rest."

"Yeah." The word exited long and breathy as he seemed to deflate into his chair.

They were quiet for a bit. And he just appreciated not being stuck in bed. But he had a lot of questions about the lady at his side.

After glancing in her direction and away and back again enough times, she turned to him. "What?"

"I didn't think I'd see you again." That's again, not what he had planned to say.

"For at least six months. I might have seen you at a board meeting."

"Oh right. True, I suppose. I'm really hoping not to return to DC." He hadn't told anyone from that town his plans. But with the purchase of his land and rodeo picking up again, he was going to let his dad know sometime. But with this injury… He stopped his thoughts before they could continue. He would not accept that rodeo was over for him. He could not.

"What are you gonna do?"

"I just bought some land. There are some cows on there

now. If I can, I'll keep up with rodeo and work the land. I'm looking at my options."

She nodded and there was such a light of understanding in her eyes he wasn't sure what to make of it. Didn't she love what she did? Wasn't she a political icon out there? His dad had said something about, "well respected on the Hill." How could she possibly understand or appreciate his need to be as far away from that life as possible? He turned away, tired. Then his eyes closed.

She said nothing more.

And he must have fallen asleep. When he opened his eyes again, she was gone. And the space around him felt lonely.

Chapter 10

Eden wanted to go home. And then she wanted to stay here forever. She thought she might see a softer side of Reid. And then she knew it was just the concussion talking. In truth, he might not even remember any of their conversation.

But she'd seen such a vulnerability there and had been so stunned to learn he might never return to Virginia. Shocked and…sad. Had a part of her hoped that she would yet be able to see him in her part of the world?

She knocked on Kellie's door. They were meeting for her follow-up evaluation.

Kellie's warm smile was always such a boost to her mood.

"Come in, Eden."

Eden sat in an overstuffed armchair across from Kellie.

Once she was settled, Kellie put all the paperwork down and met her gaze. "I have to say last night was so fun. The guys really took to you."

"They're nice. You're right. Good men. Respectful."

"And you spent some time with Reid too, this afternoon. Given your experience, what do you think about his ability to ride again?" Kellie's eyes showed her how concerned she was about Reid's future in rodeo.

"I can't tell, of course. He is responding similarly to some concussion victims and differently from others. No one is the same with this." She sat back. "With any luck he will be spared the emotional side effects I've been feeling."

"Yes, let's talk about that."

As Eden thought about what had been really bothering her lately, all the emotions that were erratic or unexplained, she poured them out as if on the desk in front of Kellie, and some of her stress about everything lessened. She saw herself in a different light. "I think what I need is just to let go." The phrase surprised her.

"Let go of what?"

Eden thought for a moment, and then was seized by a memory she'd long since pushed aside. It's not like she forgot it ever, but it was there in the back of her memories as one of the horrors of war. She'd told herself over and over that everyone had memories they wished they could forget. Everyone tried not to dwell on things that made them sad, but in this case, this memory was worse for her.

She couldn't meet Kellie's eyes and suddenly all she wanted to do was get out of that office, get outside and run. Run anywhere for a long, long time. Run until she understood this flood of thoughts and memories. The children, the explosion. The one boy, his young scared eyes. The deafening silence after the shrapnel settled, checking for blood. Feeling her limbs. Holding him close, so close, like if she held him tightly enough, she could squeeze the life back into him. Her heart tore in two, as if separating at a weak spot she'd not noticed before. Guilt. "I think I need to let go." The sobs that poured out of her came without thought and Kellie was up and resting a hand on her shoulder as soon as they started. "It's my fault. And there's nothing I can do..." Her crying ebbed, but the sorrowful emptiness continued. "I can't fix it." She looked up, taking the tissue that Kellie offered and then was unsure where to look, what to say. She hadn't known those feelings were there, hadn't realized she'd been dealing with so much guilt, and now that it was all here in front of them both, she wasn't sure what to do about it.

Kellie pressed her hand down on Eden's shoulder with a stronger weight, as if the effort would infuse more strength, and it did. Eden felt her courage rise, felt her desire to change increase. She wanted to know what to do. She wanted to face this. As terrifying as it was.

Kellie moved back to her chair. "That came as a surprise, didn't it?"

Eden nodded. "I—I'm not sure what to do with this."

"I think you're right. I think you can let that go. You honor the lives lost by living your own."

Thinking back on the memories that had torn through her, Eden knew she couldn't just let them go as simply as someone suggested. They had to be clung to, held close, or something. She'd done the same for so long. "But the children. They were innocent." Her panic at deserting them, at forgetting their memory caused her limbs to tremble. "And the others." Her commander, the men in her squadron, the soldiers with her, forced her to leave even the injured children. "They're going to die." The words hung in her thoughts as a beacon, a warning and now a condemnation. Could she desert them twice? In their moment of death and in their memory?

"Have you given them a memorial?"

Confused she shook her head. "I…I don't think the Iraqis gave funerals. We certainly weren't invited."

Kellie pulled out an old binder, well read and used, and she scooted over closer to Eden so that she could see. "Take a look at some of these."

Eden wasn't sure what she was seeing at first. A painting, a sculpture. A bonfire. A signed t-shirt. But then a picture of a scrapbook-looking book with the title, "Letting Go," clued her in. "People's memorials?"

Kellie nodded, and Eden was surprised to see tears in her eyes. "Each one the heartfelt memories of their past. The honor in the difficult times that they most desperately couldn't let go of, because it deserved a place, a memory." She turned the pages, one at a time.

Something very right about this book filled her. The children. They could be honored, remembered, cherished, but it didn't have to be inside Eden. "But what can I do?" She didn't have much artistic talent; she wasn't, in fact, very creative at all.

"You'll know. It has to be something that works inside of you, something that will project all your feelings of responsibility, all your memories, all your love for these children, onto something that will keep it for you."

"Keep it for me." The idea was so freeing, so incredibly lifting, that despite her earlier crying, she was now soaring with a new sense of love she'd never felt before. A love that was perhaps begun at first by acceptance. Fix this. And that was something she hadn't experienced in a long time. Acceptance.

"I went to Iraq to serve my country. I went out of love."

Kellie nodded and leaned forward. "Go on."

"But when I got there, love made me do hateful things. Serving the country, keeping my squadron safe, that meant others had to die. To suffer." She swallowed. There was more to it than that, but somehow uttering those words helped her see more than she ever had.

"What you did is more than almost everyone you ever meet will appreciate. They don't look at you and see the sacrifice you made, not really. They don't understand, and they couldn't appreciate it if you explained it. But it's inside you and I think as you find a way…to express just precisely what was going on inside, you can keep it safe and outside. And maybe even you will understand. Or the ones you love." She pointed to a drawing. It was of a baby, wrapped tightly after birth, with the serenity of a newborn and she could see the great love and care that was taken in even the tiniest wrinkles on her new skin and then below, "Gone. I'm sorry."

Somehow those words spoke to Eden more than others. She knew she was going to have to do something similar. But what? There was no way she could capture by drawing any of those children, the last looks she saw on their faces, the fear, the looks of the betrayed youth. Those looks had haunted her for all this time.

"Do you write?"

"Hm?"

"Do you ever journal? Or write?"

She had written journals all through her youth and even into college. It was just when she went into the military, with so few possessions and so little time that she stopped. And, she admitted, she'd no desire to remember some of the things that happened in her day. "I used to love it."

"Do you think it would help to detail every bit you remember? Every thing that haunts you? Pour it out on the page."

"And then what?" She didn't think she could bear to ever read it.

"Then it will be there. Remembered. The journal will keep it for you."

Eden started nodding, slowly at first, and then with more focus. "Yes. I think I could try." She shuddered at the thought.

"You don't have to do it all at once. You certainly don't need to be pressured to even complete it while you are here, but I think it would help in your case in particular."

Eden suspected she was right. She loved this idea of something else caring for her responsibilities, for the memories. "I'll try."

"Do you have a journal you think would work? Sometimes people like to choose the journal carefully. And sometimes it becomes a place they put all kinds of heartbreaks that might come."

"I think I'll run into town to look and see if I can find one."

Kellie nodded and put the book away. "Can I ask a favor of you?"

Surprised, Eden nodded. "Of course."

"Could you take Reid into town with you?"

A flush of shock and a wave of pleasure rose up inside. "Um. Okay. Do you think he'd want to go?"

"To get out of here? Oh yeah. But I need you to keep him away from the fairgrounds. No rodeo for him, just all the other things town has to offer. Maybe get something to eat. Ask him to show you all their old hangouts. Maybe go out to the dunes."

She had no idea what dunes these might be or what the town could possibly offer, but she was game to try, if Kellie thought it would be important. "Do you think he should ride again?"

"He will. Whether or not he should is the question most on our minds. Should he ride again? Is it worth permanent damage to his brain? Is that even a risk here?" Kellie shrugged. "I know this meeting and these weeks at Broken Hearts Ranch are about you, but I can't help but think there is more going on here, a larger purpose for you. And I know for sure Reid could really use the help."

Eden didn't totally hold to similar feelings about fate, but she was impressed once again with the depth of Kellie's love for the guys, for the feeling of family there.

"You all have something special here. I've never felt anything like it. Well, except with my military brothers and sisters." And for the first time in a while, Eden remembered again not the domineering hard leaders, but the sibling love that existed between her and many of the others. She realized she hadn't talked to them in a long time, hadn't reached out, had probably rebuffed their efforts to maintain closeness. "I bet the other people in my squadron are suffering from these same types of things."

Kellie nodded, "Certainly. Whether or not they are seeking help, I don't know, but how could they not be?"

Eden determined to get them all together at least over their conference call in the next week or so. Perhaps these new thoughts might help one of them as well.

As she left Kellie's office this time, she was excited to get going. She knew that writing these things down, preserving the memories, might be the most freeing thing she'd done to heal. And just the thought of doing so was healing parts of her broken heart already.

They had decided that Eden was going to try to leave as soon as possible to go into town. She went in search of

Reid, but he was not where she had left him. She smiled at the chair he had fallen asleep in. A sleeping Red was an entirely different person than a live and in command Reid. Or maybe it was the therapy talking. She was more comfortable with herself. And the person asleep at her side had seemed so vulnerable, so unsure, so looking to her for help and hope that her heart had softened towards him. Hopefully this nicer, softer side to Reid would stay. Now, the thought of going to town with the man was appealing.

She found him back in his room. Tracey held a water bottle up to his mouth. "Open."

"What?"

"Open. I'll squirt some in."

He closed his eyes. "I think I'm good."

"I saw you outside on the porch. And I just knew you must be thirsty. I don't know why Eden didn't bring you anything to drink, and then she just left you there. Did you make it back to your room ok? Do you want some food?"

As soon as Eden was within eyesight, Reid's gaze connected with her own and she bit the inside of her cheek to keep from laughing. "You ready?"

He stepped down to the floor. "Yes." His lack of even asking "for what" made her smile and warmed her heart.

"You'll need shoes."

"Done." But the fatigue that filled his face as he stared down at his boots brought out all Eden's sympathy. "But I'm gonna need some help with my boots." His smile was part embarrassed and part challenge. And she was always up for a challenge, but wouldn't he be more comfortable in easier shoes? "Do we have slides or sandals or even a pair of Nikes?"

"Not here. And I always wear my boots when I'm in

Texas. I can't be seen going to Roosters in a pair of Nikes." His gaze lingered to send his point home.

Ryan stepped up beside Eden and she jumped. "Ryan!"

"Yep, I'm here. Sorry to make you jump. I'll grab your boots."

"Thanks, man."

Eden reached for them when Ryan returned, but Tracey snatched them first and knelt in front of Reid. He almost shooed her away, but then sat back in exhaustion.

"Hold up your foot."

Eden covered her mouth and turned to hide her laugh.

But Reid just leaned back with a small smile on his face. It was a testament to how tired he was that he just let her wrestle with his boots. She helped him to stand and walked him all the way to Ryan's truck. They stopped only once to ease the dizziness.

Reid pulled out his own keys. "Can we stop by my truck too? I'd like to get it jump started and back up to the house."

"Of course."

Tracey closed the door for him and Eden bit back her laugh all the way down to the tree lining that surrounded the house and then she let go just a little. "So, do you have a new friend?"

"Not another word." His face was pale, but his determination seemed to have spread. "Where are we going? I don't even care where it is, but I'm curious."

"We're buying me a journal."

"Pardon me?"

She nodded. "Yep. If that sounds too boring for you, you're welcome to stay."

"Nope. That's great." The speed of his answer made her laugh again.

"And of course, picking up your truck, but actually, you can't drive, so maybe not. And Kellie told me to ask you about some of the stuff you guys did in college around here. Apparently, she thinks it would be good for me to get out, see the sights; might be healing for me." Eden knew she was fibbing just a little. Kellie was hoping for this to benefit Reid, but as she talked, she knew that it would also be good for her. Maybe the unlikely pair could make something of this time in Texas and help each other out. And something about Reid was growing on her more and more.

"Hey, I'm seriously just happy to be outside the house."

She tried to swallow back a ping of discomfort that the only reason this might be enjoyable for him was so that he could get out of the house. Of course that would be most on his mind, and she was kidding herself if he was going to think this anything other than a health mission. Which is exactly what she thought it was. But it still felt like a jab that he was not thinking of anything else, not even friendship.

He directed her into town. When they got there, she reached for her handle. "Now, you just stay put. I'll run in and come back out."

"What? No ma'am. *You* stay put. I'll be getting your door and we can both run in and run out."

The fact that he would be running nowhere lingered in the air around them. Their walk into the store would be slow at best. But she just nodded. Sometimes it was important to be able to do the little things, when all the big things were drifting away.

When he stood at her door, he smiled. And she knew she was right in thinking he needed this usefulness. She stood close while they walked across the parking lot into the nearest bookstore. He grinned. "This place is great." He held the door open for her. The place looked small on the outside, but wow, when she entered, she could tell that the owner used every space, every wall, and that a great amount of care went into the space. She was immediately enchanted. "I wanted to own a bookstore once." As she said the words, the old longing returned.

"I can see that."

She turned to him. Was he teasing her?

His eyes were sincere, and it looked like maybe he was trying to compliment her. Okay, she'd take it.

"Yes, I dreamed of each space and a small corner with chairs for the kids. And a stage. With dress up clothes." She stopped blurting out all the other small details she'd imagined about the space. But seeing a store that could so easily fit that one in her dreams had brought them all immediately back into her mind. This trip was surprising her in every way.

If he wondered about the stage, he didn't say anything. "So what are you looking for?" Reid's question brought her out of her bookstore reverie, and she walked with him over to the wall of what looked like journals. "Something to write in."

He carefully lowered himself into the nearest chair. "Can I sit here while we decide?"

We? Was he going to help her? She studied him and made a decision. Perhaps she could share a vague version of her task today. "I need a place I can write memories that are better left outside my brain." She didn't know if he would get it, but he took it in stride apparently and then said, "So you're gonna have to love it, but you might hate it sometimes. But it will be precious to you."

"Yes, exactly. And it has an important job to do."

"What is its job?"

"To memorialize those who deserve to be remembered, but the thoughts are too painful."

He reached out his hand.

She wasn't exactly sure what he wanted, but she offered hers.

He took it in his and captured it with both hands, almost like a hand-held embrace, and every nerve reactor shot bursts of pleasure up her arm. What on earth?

"I'd stand like a real man and hug that pain out of you, but this is all I got right now."

She was stunned.

He shrugged. "Maybe later when I'm back to myself." His slight insecurity melted her a bit more.

"Thank you." She turned from him before she said something more about how nice a real hug would feel sometime. Just him mentioning one brought such a yearning for what he called a "real man" hug that she almost trembled for it. She'd learned tender things today. She'd planned to do hard things. She'd also put a man in bed with a concussion. She was facing memories that she'd buried deep and it was all a bit much. She was way more needy than she'd been in a long time.

She wiped at her eye and then walked along the wall, clearing her throat. "So I need to find something that I will cherish and hate and want to keep forever." She tapped her chin. Not an easy decision.

"What about that one?" He pointed to a shelf down by her foot. She crouched. "Which one?" And then she saw it. Sensible. Pretty. She lifted a light blue soft leather journal in her hands. "This." She turned to him. "This is the one." She searched his face. How could he know such a thing?

"That's the one I would want to write in if I were you."

She tucked it under her arm and then on impulse asked, "Which one do you want?"

He looked surprised for a second, but then pointed to the one next to the light blue. "How about that brown one there?"

It was heavier in her hands. And more rugged. She imagined him packing it with his things, and it seemed to fit. "I'll just go buy these. Stay put."

He tipped his hat. "Yes, ma'am."

She laughed and then realized he probably wasn't even acting. This was the cowboy code. They were respectful. Treated their women right and worked hard. How could she not see any of this in him while they were out in DC?

Her head shook in confusion all the way to the register. How could a person be one way in one state and completely different in another? Well, she was about to spend a lot of time with a person she had earlier hoped to never see again, and she would find out.

Chapter 11

Reid watched Eden at the register. He'd gotten a stream of texts a mile long about how great this woman was and how he'd better take care of her and don't be messing with her mind and did he know she'd even served in Iraq. He'd never felt so teamed up on with The Chute.

Does anyone remember I'm stuck here and not on my horse?

You complaining about sleeping in a house full of women?

Yep.

Well I'm crying a river.

I'm doing the mini violin thing.

Where should I take Eden? Reid needed to redirect these clowns.

Like on a date?

The kissy emoji made him laugh.

Kellie thought it would be a good idea for her to relax around town.

Eden had said it was for him, but he knew the truth. She didn't know it, but Kellie wanted him to help Eden relax, have a good time, forget whatever was plaguing her. He could do that. If he could walk without passing out.

The guys starting throwing out old hangouts, all their favorite things to do when they were bored. And most of them were ridiculous.

But really, take her to the overlook.

He nodded to himself. Now that would be something she would appreciate. And if she needed to talk to someone, he was a good listener. He couldn't move.

And a shake at O'Malleys.

Of course. No one has lived here unless they've had O'Malleys.

Don't forget Mariah's Bakery.

By the time Eden had purchased her journal, and his, he had a whole day planned.

"Where to now?" Eden held the bag with her journal close.

"Do you want to start writing?"

"What?" She looked down at her bag. "Kind of?"

"We could do that. I know just the place."

"And you're not really mobile anyway, right?"

"Not really, no. What we need are some trees."

"We do?"

"Certainly. You can't write your life's secrets down without trees."

She didn't look convinced, but they climbed into the truck and she looked to him. But he was searching around in the glove box and then in the area underneath his seat and behind them. "Aha!" He held up the portable hammocks the guys used all summer their freshmen year.

"Oh, that's a great idea!"

"Ok, drive on, chauffeur. I'll find us some trees."

"Before we get to our final destination, we need to go to O'Malleys."

"That sounds kind of Irish for a small Texas town."

"Oh, it is. And they take great pride in their roots. They also make the best shakes I've ever had. We can grab some burgers and shakes to take with us."

"Sustenance for our journey."

"Exactly. I don't know how long it's gonna take for you to write your life in that book."

"Do you even know what I'm writing?"

"Well, no, but by the time most people have reached our age, a lot of life has happened, right?"

"True. I don't know what to say. Maybe I'll share some of what this is supposed to do for me." She nudged him. "You write too."

"I'm game." They drove to O'Malleys, picked up the food through the new drive-through option, and then he had her head off the main road and onto a country road that soon turned to dirt. Finally, they were climbing up the only hill in town, the only hill for miles.

Once they'd parked, she attached the first hammock. There were two sets of trees close enough that they would be near each other. He tugged on the hammock to make sure it was secured before getting inside. "So I guess this is what rodeo guys do when they're injured? Glad the trees are close together. It would be nice to talk too, you know?"

Soon they were swinging side by side in their hammocks, looking out over the farther parts of the valley below. As it got darker, he planned to show her the very edge and they would see the twinkling lights below and the stars above. The best part about this view was actually the stars above. So many more were visible here. He couldn't wait to see her face when they came out.

The pen she handed him felt heavy. What was he supposed to write with this?

"So, this is your book to put all your heartbreaks or your complaints, your angers even. It's not meant to be read, ever. It's meant to collect this negativity from you and keep it for you. Memorialize the good and safeguard the bad so that it doesn't have to stay inside. Write as many details as you can so that it's there, being taken care of for you."

He considered her words. "Did Kellie tell you all that?"

"She suggested it. And it made so much sense to me, I felt something right here in my center. I know I need to do this." She dug around in her bag and pulled out tissues. "But this is not going to be easy. Just remember that you suggested we come." Her joke fell a bit flat and her laugh sounded stale. But she seemed to rally. "Anyway. I'm not sure how much I'll be able to write tonight. It's going to be hard. But I'll stop when I can't go further. Kellie said it could take a long time."

He nodded. "I could drum up all kinds of disappointed stares from my father to write about in here."

She laughed, then pointed her pen at him. "I think it will come to mind if it needs to go in there. It's uncanny how it just starts to flow. I have lots of things to deal with from my time in Iraq, way more than I realized."

Thinking about her over there, fighting, the guns. It turned his stomach. "When I met you, I didn't think women went to war. I mean, I knew theoretically there were women who did, but seeing you, hearing your bio, knowing about your organization, it made it real to me." He pressed his lips together so he wouldn't say more. She didn't need his moralizing on the subject.

"You don't like it?"

"Like what? That women go to war?" He shook his head. "No, I don't."

She studied him for a while before answering. And he guessed she came up against his way of thinking a lot. He braced himself for a challenge. But instead, she just looked back at her journal. "I can respect that. From you, I'll take that reaction."

"I'm honored, but surprised." He wanted to ask what changed, because he didn't think she would have taken anything from him when he met her. But he didn't want to bring up her earlier disdain for him, because she clearly did not like him during their time in DC.

"There is a place for a woman who wants to serve her country." She continued to stare at her journal.

"I guess I'd just much rather see you safe. I'd rather a man step in harm's way so that you don't have to. I was not raised by a cowboy, but Dad sure as heck drilled into me that women are cherished, protected, and provided for."

She sighed and it wasn't a frustrated or tired sigh, but a wistful one. Could it be that she wished for the same in her life?

"That sounds nice. I wouldn't begrudge you your opportunity to do that for a woman as long as you don't begrudge me mine."

"Understood. My desire to protect you shouldn't keep you sheltered away."

"Exactly."

"Understood." How different their conversation was now from before. "I'm sorry for the stuff you had to see there."

They sat in silence for a moment and then scratches on her notepad sounded in his ears. So he started his own entry.

He was lost to all sounds after a time as he relived memories with his dad. He expected to be disturbed by them, to be angrily scratching out his own emotions, but the surprise came as he found most of his thoughts enjoyable. He found lots of evidence of his dad's love, of shared experiences, and of times when he and his dad had been very similar.

Her sniffles interrupted.

He braved a glance, and the crumpled defeat he saw etched on her face tore at him. He shifted in his hammock to face her. "No. Oh no. You do not have to do this."

She nodded, sniffing. Her face fell in her hands. "Yes, I do."

Nope. This was not gonna do. He stood. "Eden."

She didn't answer but the dejection in her shoulders, the pain that seemed to hover around her, showed no signs of easing.

"Now, I can't stand it when a lady cries." He approached her side. "You don't have to do this alone. May I?" He indicated he'd like to get in her hammock behind her. He wasn't sure what she'd say but asked without thinking first. As was his way with her apparently.

She just nodded and sat up.

Gingerly he climbed in, hoping not to overturn them both.

The thing wobbled, it dipped, and it sunk lower to the earth, but eventually his legs were stretched out on either side of her and her back rested up against him.

His arms wrapped around her as if they were made to do such a thing. He didn't say anything at first, but the way she melted into him eased whatever awkwardness he might have created. His instincts had been correct. She needed the closeness. His chin rested on the top of her head and they sat in silence. He could do this for her. While he didn't know her very well, he knew what she needed, and he could be that. Why he was the one or why he could, he didn't even think about right now. It felt…nice to be the one she turned to.

After a time, he asked, "Do you want to keep writing?"

Her pain tugged at him. But her light smell of…mint, the softness of her skin under his arms, the perfect way she fit against his chest were starting to do things to him. He knew his heartrate started to pick up, and he did everything he could to slow it down. The pounding would soon be obvious.

She shifted so that he could see her face. "Can I talk to you?"

He knew she didn't mean simple conversation. What he was about to hear was gonna be a little raw.

Her eyes beamed with trust, a feeling he knew he couldn't possibly deserve, but he determined to rise and be whatever it was she thought him to be.

"I promise not to mansplain anything."

She laughed, a light, short rumble in her back he felt along his chest. And the moment was so intimate, one he wouldn't normally have shared with her unless they were much more physically close, but it created a feeling of trust in him as well. Would he also share?

As she turned back to face the valley out in front of them, an eagle hovered, floating on the currents. He envied those birds. Rodeo did that for him. Gave him that feeling of freedom. But would he always be able to ride? This injury showed him the reality of his profession. No. He would not. And for the first time in his life, he'd begun to wonder, what next? Land purchasing had come at a good time, but it wasn't a complete plan.

Her soft fingers brushed against his arms as she lifted her journal again and her pen. "I do think this will help me." A deep breath filled her, pressing her further back into him. "But I'd like to talk."

He waited, imagining the strength it must take to open up.

"There was a boy."

She kept talking, her words flowing out just loud enough for him to hear. And he listened. The more he heard, the more astounded he was at the sorrows of war. The more his admiration for this small woman in his arms grew. The tighter he wanted to enfold her in his arms and never let go.

"He was injured by the same blast that gave me my concussion." Her voice started shaking, and he knew she was sharing some of the most painful and private moments of her life. "I know I could have saved him. I chose duty over love, or something." She sighed. "I anguish over that."

"Maybe a different kind of love?"

She nodded. "I've thought of that. Love for country, love for Americans, love for this one boy. It's all love." Her body tensed. "But how could it be right to leave him?" She shook her head.

"It wasn't."

She whipped around so fast to look into his face, she almost dumped them both on the ground. He spread out his body to steady the hammock. "Before you get all in my face about this, I'm saying this as tenderly as possible." His eyes pled with hers to understand. She studied him a moment, not quite suspicious, mostly surprised and wary.

"It wasn't right to leave him. It wasn't right to stay with him either. It wasn't right to bomb and kill other humans. It wasn't right for the dictator to take over and mistreat his citizens. It wasn't right that you had to go to make peace at all. So much wasn't right about all of that. What was your other choice? You desert your squadron you'd sworn to protect, desert your country and die at the side of a child who was about to die?" His throat suddenly filled, and moisture filled his eyes. The pain in his heart was unbearable for a moment, thinking of what she'd just told him, thinking that she, this soft small woman, had had to live through that. That no one had stepped in to shield her. He wanted to back up time and stand at her side, be the barrier to all the danger, the evils, the awful sights. The pain was not sitting well at the moment either. He wanted to stand up, run, turn away, process everything she'd just told him by himself, but it wasn't even his pain. So he sat very, very still and bore it with her, because that's what he'd said he would do.

"I see his face in my dreams sometimes. Not so much lately, but he's there." She lifted her journal. "And now he's in here."

He nodded, knowing she could feel his head behind her. He tried to appear calm. But inside he was a thunderstorm in Texas, raging all its fury on the unsuspecting prairie. And all he wanted to be was the pavilion, the place of refuge and peace. He wanted to be sure this brave warrior woman never had to feel anything like that ever again.

Chapter 12

Eden knew Reid was crying. He didn't shudder or sniff or wipe his eyes, but she knew. He cried for her. And the empathy that flowed between them, this beautiful sorrow that he shared in her memory was the most healing thing that had happened to her. Was it the writing in the journal? Was it the talking, the opening up? She couldn't know, but the feeling of unity was beautiful and she wanted it again. And again. How utterly strange that it would come from Reid Browning of all people. She corrected herself. The person she thought Reid Browning was. They sat in the hammock together for more minutes of silence than talking, but those minutes…each one served its purpose.

She didn't think she could write any more as afternoon turned into dusk. She'd addressed the toughest memory. And she was ready to set it aside until next time she pulled out the journal. And she was aware of every increase in the pounding of his heart at her back. Every shift of his body, every ripple across his stomach. The closeness, and the intense emotion had left her bare and wanting. Needing his arms, his touch, needing him. Just as she was about to suggest they walk to the edge to see the view, before she did something she might regret, Reid lifted his hand and using one finger, traced her hairline. A shiver of pleasure ran through her and she knew she was in trouble if she wanted to avoid the entanglement of anything physical with this new Reid. But instead of physically taking it any further, he began to talk, his finger tracing lines down her head, driving her to distraction. The sensation was overpowering in many ways and comforting at the same time. He probably had no idea the effect his seemingly unplanned touch had caused.

"My dad and I aren't close." His voice rumbled through her.

"Mm." She wanted him to keep talking, but she didn't know what to say, what he needed.

"He always wanted me to be a lawyer. He wanted me to go to Yale. He wanted me to play football. He wanted…" He laughed, a sort of humorless ironic sound. "Perhaps you're seeing the pattern."

She nodded.

"Well, I played football. And I'm glad. I met some of my best friends, including the guy who introduced me to rodeo. I went to law school. Harvard."

She waited, unsure if he was even talking to her anymore or speaking aloud to the evening sky. Either way, she felt like it was about to become important for him, if her own experience was any indication.

"But I also entered the local small town rodeo outside of Dallas, kind of on a whim, to join this new friend. It was the bareback." He shook his head. "I thought, anyone can stay on a horse for eight seconds."

"Did you?"

"No way. I got bucked off in less than one. And that's when I knew I had to conquer this."

"I hear you're nationally ranked, about to start a tour?"

"Yes, but winning isn't always the same as conquering something."

"What is?"

"I don't know exactly." His breath left his chest in a long deep exhale. She felt like she sunk closer and closer to him as his chest lowered. "When will I know if I'm done?" He lifted one of her hands and each touch, each absent-minded lift of a finger sent a thrill of expectation through her. "What if I never ride again?" Something shuddered through him and she didn't turn to invade his privacy. "What if that practice run I did a few days ago was my last bareback ride?" He brought one of her fingers to his mouth. Then he laced their hands together.

The wind had picked up and the sun was almost to the horizon.

"I know I can't ride forever. I picked one sport you definitely age out of, sooner rather than later. But what am I gonna do when this is all over? I refuse to think my father was right. But just like he's always said, I'm injured. I'll get injured again. If I'm not finished now, I will be one day. And then what?"

"You're not aged out yet. Maybe you have started thinking about this early enough that you can prepare, maybe set up a life for yourself for after." She didn't really know what he had planned, what rodeo people made as far as salary or what expectations he could have for a career. From what she could tell listening to everyone, all six guys graduated from the local community college. But he had his law degree.

He didn't answer her. She didn't expect him to. These

sounded like thoughts that would not be solved in one sitting. "Let's go see my land."

The words came out without warning, and for a minute, she wasn't sure he was serious. "Now?"

"No, tomorrow. Do you have time tomorrow? I know you're supposed to be participating at the ranch, doing…things."

She laughed at his obvious lack of knowledge about what they did.

"I think tomorrow we're starting real ranch duties if we would like."

"And do you want to do that? I could help with that maybe, if my head feels better."

She heard the but in that sentence. For whatever reason, he really wanted to take her out to his land.

"Where is it?"

His arms circled her again. "About an hour from here. I'll take you to the River Walk in San Antonio too, if you want, make it more fun?" The hope in his voice is what convinced her.

"I'd love to go out there." She turned to him. "Today has been a gift. The journal, you listening, everything. I'd be happy to do something similar for you if you think it would help." She'd wanted him to see the sincerity in her expression, but now that they were facing one another, and closer than ever, she realized the intensity of her new physical attraction to Reid.

His gaze travelled over her face and she at once became aware of how comfortable she felt right there in his arms.

"It will help. I need to go. And." His smile grew. "I don't want to share you with Kellie and a bunch of women." His lips twitched, and the eyes that sparkled back at her were full of humor.

"Oh, you don't?" She twisted more so that she was facing him more fully, moving inches closer to his face, almost pressing against his chest.

He took his time shaking his head no. "I don't." One hand pressed against her back, just enough as if to invite her to move closer. He waited, his eyes earnest, his mouth full. She'd expected it to be more firm looking, but the larger lower lip, the soft curve of the indent on his upper lip, the perfect separation where her mouth might fit drew her in more than she had been expecting. She adjusted herself to be closer, studying his face, her thoughts racing but none making sense, none except the one consistent desire to taste his lips. The thought had come on quickly, no doubt motivated by how close he was, by how easy it would be to kiss him. But now that it had entered her consciousness, there was no quieting the desire that rose inside permeating all the way through her.

Something in his eyes changed and the darkening, *his* desire cancelled all her resistance. She closed the distance until she felt the puff of his breath on her mouth, tickling her senses. "Reid." She whispered. Before she could think another thing, his arms tightened around her and he pressed his lips to hers. They were warm, tender, as soft as she imagined, and full of feeling. So much feeling. All that they had just shared, all the healing she had just felt, all the vulnerability they had experienced. His tears for her. The experiences rushed around them pulling them closer, uniting their minds and setting her heart on fire. This man, could he be all that she suspected he was? Were they so well suited? She responded to his insistence, returning with more of her own. Until the initial soft hesitance was replaced by a strength of desire she was unprepared for.

He growled and with his arms wrapped fully around

her, rotated her body so that his face was above her own and he pressed into her as if the desert had deprived him of water for many weeks. Over and over he captured her lips until she was lost to anything but him, the strength of his arms, his solid chest above her, and the back of his neck as she ran her hands up his arms and into his hair.

"Eden." His murmur, his voice, was almost more sexy than anything else. Her name. Eden.

"Say it again." Her lips caressed his with the words as she pulled his bottom lip in her mouth. "Say it."

"What?" The smile that interrupted her kisses frustrated her and she bit it away.

"Ow." He kissed her back, running his tongue along her mouth until she opened further for him.

They played, teased, and laughed for a few more minutes before he paused again, and she knew he was going to put a stop to things. "Eden."

"Mmm. There it is."

"Your name?" He adjusted the hair out of her face. "You're beautiful, you know. Right here, your hair splayed out everywhere. The first time I ever saw you I thought so too."

And then their first moments together came rushing back. Her frown grew before she could even mask it.

"And now you're remembering the benefit dinner."

"You were so different then."

"I was?" He shook his head. "You were." He kissed her nose—perhaps to soften the conversation.

It worked, probably because she was just as eager to return to their closeness. "You're so different than I thought you were."

His kisses trailed across her forehead and down her nose to her mouth once again. "I can't get enough of your lips."

He lingered again, caressing her mouth with such a tender longing that a tightness grew in her belly and the soft spread of tingles down to her toes created a new eagerness. But he sat up, adjusting their balance in the hammock and situated himself further away, still touching, but nowhere near her mouth.

"Do you want to go see the view?"

The night had darkened. The trees overhead blocked the moon, which lit most of the ground around them.

"You're gonna love this." He reached for her hand and then placed his feet back on the ground to steady the hammock. "But first we have to get out of this thing without breaking my head or anything on you."

She laughed as it swung out in a crazy way and he had to pull her on top of him with his feet firmly planted, in order to keep them both upright.

He stood and then pulled her up beside him. She watched his face. No evidence of dizziness seemed to plague him, he didn't wince or hold his head. Their hands linked immediately with such an ease, as if they'd been filled with their new intimacy long before now. He led her out of the trees. She thought they were heading out to the ledge but he stopped. She turned to him, searching his face.

"Look up."

She lifted her chin and then gasped. "Oh." The entire night sky was lit with beacons of light. Almost every dark space filled with stars. "Wow, is that the Milky Way?" The cloudy path across the sky was brighter and more milky than she'd ever imagined it could be.

"I knew you would love this."

She smiled and couldn't look away. "You know what's amazing? That strip of Milky Way. I never really understood what it is. Why is it milky? But then it occurred to me.

It is like the other side of the spiral." She held up her hands. "We're on one side of the spiral and it's on the other."

He lifted her hand to his lips. "You know I love that you just said that?"

"You do?" She laughed but was trying to recover from the word, love, coming out of his lips.

"Yup. I've said the exact same thing before, and people looked at me like they didn't know what I was talking about."

"It's the first thing I thought. I've always heard people talking about the Milky Way and sometimes they'd say, "See that powdery kind of spot in the sky?" She shook her head. "It just now occurred to me that those stars, even though they're far away, they're part of us. They're a part of the spiral."

He nodded as though she was speaking everything he'd thought before. How was it that they were so much alike? Were they? As their hands hung together, linked together, she followed him over to the edge and they sat on a rock outcropping, still many feet away from any drop. "See that light over there with the kind of blue glow? That's Scaggs."

She laughed. "Do I want to know what Scaggs is?"

"Only the best burgers you'll ever eat."

She watched his face. He loved Lost Creek. It was obvious with every proud movement of his head, every point of his finger. "And that over there? Mariah's. That woman is a gem. Her éclairs. I die. Every time. And way over there, that dark mass, those are the dunes. We have to go out there. You've never seen anything like it, I guarantee it."

One by one, he pointed out places in Lost Creek. All

the places they would go, their hangouts, and all the dumb things they'd done as college guys.

"I wish I'd had something like that in college. Wish I did now."

"Like what? A bunch of cowboys riding around on horses or bulls?"

"Yes, but more, a family of friends. I've never had that."

He gently bumped his shoulder against hers. "Well, you do now."

And she didn't know how, but she felt that quite possibly she did.

Chapter 13

Reid sat at Eden's side in his truck the next day on the way to and through San Antonio to his land. With still another hour to go, his truck, rescued from the back roads of Kellie's ranch, swallowed up the road, but not quickly enough. He'd signed the closing documents by fax. When they stepped out onto the soil, it would be onto his land, owned free and clear.

Eden stared out the window. The woman seemed to take everything in with the same powerful curiosity. And now that fascination was directed at the hill country of Texas. "Everything here is so peaceful. The green stretches for miles and miles, the hills rolling just enough that it's kind of hypnotic."

He smiled to himself. Watching Eden, he realized he cared how she felt about his land. "That's what I thought when I first saw it. This land has been a lot of years in the planning. But I can finally picture it. Me, on the front porch, looking out at this." He held his hand out to the green on all sides. "This view every day."

"That sounds like heaven." Her forehead wrinkled for a moment but she didn't say anything more.

"What?"

"Hm?"

"But...I feel like there's a *but* in there."

"Oh, well, no. Not for you. I just...I don't know. I think I would feel like I'm hiding here. Like it's great to be away and to rest from cares, but..." She didn't look like she wanted to continue but he waited.

"But there's work to be done. And if I hide here, none of that gets done."

He didn't answer for a long time. At first he thought she sounded a lot like his dad and that wasn't sitting well with him, but his dad was different. He worked to earn money, and there wasn't anything wrong with that either. But his billable attorney hours, his desire to see and be seen, his constant drive to stay on top, be on top made Reid tired. "See, I'm not like that. The rat race out there makes my skin crawl. I go when I have to and no more."

"I don't like that part of it either, and some of the people we might both know are cringey. I know. But a lot of good happens there too. New laws, protections, fund raising for important causes. Just last year, we helped over one thousand vets get the emotional care and support they need. We're raising education and learning more ourselves all the time."

He nodded and reached for her hand. "And I totally respect that. I feel your passion. These people, you, served our country, gave all, and are suffering from lifetime repercussions. The least we can do is get them the best help available. You're awesome, Eden. It's not that."

"Yeah, so that's what's difficult for me. This is gorgeous. And so tempting. How nice to step away from the awful parts of my job…" The eyes she turned to him were pleading for understanding.

"Right. But if you run from the awful, none of what brings you joy gets done either."

"Exactly."

And in the silence that followed, Reid wondered if this whole trip was a waste of time. He had hoped, he realized now, that in showing her the ranch, something would catch her heart like it had his and he could one day convince her to come live in Texas. The realization astounded him. He and Eden were so new. He had no idea where it could possibly go. But already he had been hoping for something long term.

"But I've got to retire someday, right?" She laughed, in a sort of forced lightheartedness.

They drove the rest of the hour toward his new land, talking of everything and nothing. It was a pleasant enough drive, but his push to convince her, his desire to experience his first steps on his own soil was muted now that he knew her heart. And did he feel right convincing her otherwise? No. She was doing a good work, doubtless helping many people, and his own father had said she was a big deal out there. Not everyone could be a big deal. He'd heard her speak. She was engaging and sympathetic, inspired trust. She was a natural.

They were about to turn left when she pointed out a small, but clean looking building in a sort of small town strip of stores. "What is that?"

The sign read, "Wounded Warriors."

"I don't know." Reid had never noticed anything like that before, but they were written on the bottom of the programs in Washington, DC.

"Aren't they a sponsor for the non-profit?"

"Maybe. Maybe they are independent." She took a picture, grabbing what looked like a phone number on the sign. "One of the biggest things we would like to do is combine efforts with all the smaller organizations, all the people already working hard for this. We will accomplish much more if we're united."

"I agree. And I know advertising is expensive, but if I knew how to easily donate, a one-time amount or monthly withdrawal, and I was reminded now and then, I think there are a lot of guys like me who would love to donate."

"Would you?"

"Of course. In fact, I can ride bareback for a cause too. I can treat it like a reverse sponsor. I obviously have my sponsors and wear their patches and clothes and use their gear, but I can include something for Vets 4 Life every time I ride, or Wounded Warrior, or whatever. To help spread the word."

"That would be amazing. Do you think the other guys might consider it too?"

"Sure. If they haven't picked a charity. Not everyone does, but we have the option. A lot of guys will just ride to help the Rodeo Association. Or Farmers of America, or something specifically linked to rodeo, but we are a patriotic bunch, and we have military nights honoring the vets in the audience. And I just know this would be a good fit." Reid's brain was already turning. "In fact, I think our bunch out here is way more into this than the elites in Washington, DC."

At her sharp questioning gaze he just waved her off. "Trust me. Wait till you see the patriotism when we sing the national anthem."

"Well okay, I'm looking forward to it then."

He was too. Especially for the nights they honored the vets. She might be moved to tears. He usually was.

"There are few things in this world I will cry over."

She leaned against the door so she could look at him. "What are they?"

"My God, my country, my family, and..." He took a moment to watch her before finishing, hoping to gauge her mood. "And my woman."

He cringed inwardly, waiting for her to come out with some jab, some tease, but when she said nothing, he braved a glance at her and saw only respect.

"You surprise me more and more. I'm not used to being surprised about a person. But you, Reid Browning, are completely different than I thought you were."

"And that's a good thing I'm assuming, since you really didn't like me before."

"That, in my opinion, is a very good thing. Wow." Her smile grew. Then she scooted back over closer to him, switched seatbelts and rested her head on his shoulder.

"Well, hey now, we're almost there. Can I get a raincheck on this situation right here?"

"For the ride home?"

"And every ride after."

"Works for me." She rested a hand on his thigh right above his knee and he cursed their closeness to his property. A part of him was tempted to take a detour. But the other part wanted to see his own place so badly, he turned down the county road as soon as he saw it. "And this is my street."

She sat up.

The road was paved, windy, somewhat narrow, and lined with gates and mailboxes. Not a house in sight. "Do people live here?"

He shrugged, "I think so? Some of them have houses

way back in. Some are about to build. And some might be like me. Not sure about the immediate future."

"Did I tell you my parents are building in Lost Creek?"

He couldn't even stop the happy grin that must have filled his face. "Do you know what that means?"

She shook her head slowly. "No."

"It means, little lady, that you and I are both gonna be calling Lost Creek home."

She laughed but she didn't deny his words, and that surprised him. Maybe she was warming up to the place. Maybe she already loved it. He just couldn't believe a woman who liked living out there in Virginia would also like a place like Lost Creek.

Then he slowed. "But here we are." He stopped at the street to give the best view. His gate was set further in, but the whole front of the property was lined with fencing, newly painted and well cared for. The grass had been trimmed. "The blue bonnets will be in bloom in about one month. I hear the whole front of the property is covered with them."

She was silent, but her hands were clasped together and when she turned to him, her eyes were shining. "This." She swallowed. "This would be difficult to ever leave."

And that right there was worth his whole drive. He clicked his remote they'd sent him and the gate opened. Then he and Eden drove down the front drive together, closing the gate with a click behind them.

"Maybe you can help me decide where we should build the house."

"Oh! I'd love that. How big is this land?"

"I've got around three hundred acres. But the space right around where the house will be is five acres of pasture land and about ten more behind. Then behind that, it's all my land further back."

"That's incredible."

He nodded. "I'm considering other plots. Eventually I would like to own most of the property surrounding mine and beyond."

"Have you decided what you'll do on it?"

"Crops. Cows. To start. Beyond that, I don't know. The land is going for a good deal. Eventually I could develop, I suppose. I think that happens to most good plots. But I'd like to have a decent sized ranch for my children to have, even if I develop some of it."

"You've got a great thing here, Reid." The approval all over her face was another reward.

"I think so too." He opened her door and held out his hand. "And hearing you say it makes everything even better."

She smiled, then let him help her hop down. "Let's go explore this land of yours."

They needed to do some of it by foot and, of course, the truck could drive most. But he led her back toward the center of the property. "We need to be aware of the trees. I don't want to cut down the large healthy old trees, especially not the live oak or the pecan, or any fruit tree in here."

"It's remarkably clear though. That's good, right?"

"I think at one point the front part of the property was excavated to prepare for a build, which never happened."

He held her hand, more out of a desire to share the experience than anything. The connection felt important. He couldn't believe how close he felt to this person who he'd hardly known, let alone liked, only a week ago.

They walked the perimeter of the close ten acres, and

both agreed on the perfect placement of the house. The drive would come in and circle in front of the home. It would be set back enough for privacy but visible from the road. A feeling of being nestled in trees with space to see the surrounding land would give him that deep satisfying feeling that came whenever he was out on the land. They took a break in their planning, standing right where he'd decided the front porch would begin. "Hold that thought." He held up a finger and then jogged out to his truck.

"You sure you should be jogging?"

"I'm fine. Head doesn't even hurt." And it was true. The dizziness was gone, at least for now. He reached in the back bed of his truck and lugged the cooler out, tucked a blanket under his arm, and jogged back to Eden.

"I could have helped." She stepped forward, reaching for the blanket.

"Now, we have to be careful about fire ants."

"Oh?" She looked around, lifting her foot to check the dirt.

"They might swarm in even if we don't see a mound. But see this rock?" He led her to a large limestone. "We have a better chance of survival on this."

"Sounds good."

"And if this doesn't work, we'll eat in the back of my truck."

"So you brought us lunch?" She laughed and hurried to him to help carry one of the bags.

"A picnic. Sure." He couldn't help but appreciate her zest for life. The simplest things brought out her smiles. He could really love having someone like that at his side. She was different from anyone he had ever spent time with.

Two surprising thoughts battled in his mind. Maybe she belonged with him. Or she belonged helping the vets in the world. Either way, someone lost. Even by the end of a filled afternoon on his property, neither thought had come out ahead of the other.

He went to sleep that night, still at Kellie's, pondering over the very problem of whether or not to encourage her life in DC or try to win her over to his place in Texas. He knew one thing for certain. If he continued to spend time with her, he'd eventually do everything in his power to convince her to stay, Washington, DC or no.

Chapter 14

Over the next week, Eden spent her mornings with Reid out on the back covered porch. Sometimes they wrote in journals. Sometimes they read. Sometimes they just talked. They didn't share the contents of their journals again. But the understanding, the unity she felt with him was undeniable. He was a part of her journey to healing. He'd become important to her in that way, and maybe more. She definitely thought of his kisses every time she looked in his direction. Did he notice the direction of her gaze? Would he kiss her again?

She blushed later one day, thinking of it while in group therapy.

"Something you'd like to share, Eden?" Kellie stood at the front, with a marker in hand at the dry erase board. She was teaching a really helpful workshop on the stress cycle, but obviously Eden's thoughts were elsewhere.

"She's just wishing Reid was in here for the workshop."

Kellie wiped her hands on the front of her jeans,

replacing the cap on her marker. "As a matter of fact, Reid will be joining us today. He's going to share his experiences riding bareback with us."

Eden commanded herself to keep a straight face. She knew the other women were watching for evidence of another blush.

But she kept herself in control so much that even when he walked into the room, and every woman fluttered to attention at the sight of him, she was able to smile naturally in response to his greeting.

Steady, Eden. After their trip to his land, she'd felt every array of emotion. Desire to move in next door, or better yet, move in, guilt for having those feelings, betrayal that she would just leave every vet to their own devices, hope that Reid wanted to spend the rest of his life with her, despair that she couldn't possibly do that, embarrassment that she'd assume such a thing. They hadn't even dated. And on and on. Now, she just hoped to hold it together long enough to listen intelligently to whatever he had to say.

"Ladies." His grin was warm and she could almost feel the ladies preen. "Let's talk about stress." He picked up the marker but instead of using it, just pulled off the cap and put it back on, over and over.

Eden didn't hear much of what he said for the next few minutes while she watched that marker and cap. It clicked every time. And she wondered if he was going to get marker on his hands. And it was one of those repetitive noises that just started to grate on a person. Whatever it was, Kellie must have found it equally distracting because she cleared her throat. "Hey, Reid, can I borrow that marker for a sec?"

"What? Oh, sure." He handed it off. "I'm not going to use that thing."

She nodded and winked at Eden.

"So, as I was saying. If you can cut down on some of the feminine drama, there will be a lot less stress in your life—"

"Excuse me? What was that?" Had Eden missed something here?

The other ladies were nodding and smiling, some even taking notes.

"If you were paying attention to what I was saying…" He winked.

But she refused to be charmed. "When you say feminine drama, what are you talking about there?"

Tracey turned around to roll her eyes at Eden. "Oh you know, like PMS, women can be cray cray."

"Uh. Hmm. So, let's think about that for a minute. So the testosterone pride that governs most warfare decisions, the face-offs between major world leaders stubbornly clinging to saving face instead of saving lives, the men who have to win and be right and did I say win? So much that no concessions are made, no compromise. That kind of feminine drama? Think of the main countries at war right now, and tell me if their leaders are women. No?" She crossed her arms. "Perhaps we want to rephrase *feminine* drama and just say, *all* drama." She didn't have to belabor the point. She could have just let it pass. She knew what he meant. All women knew what it meant. But, to watch a tall arrogant man stand up at the front lecturing them on feminine drama was too much for her sensibilities. She'd been putting up with male drama for long enough. And she wasn't about to let the comment slide. She stood and stared down into his face.

He studied her for a moment and then nodded his head. "Case in point."

"What!" She stepped closer to him at the front.

"Well, here right now, for example. I'm teaching a workshop, mention the word feminine and drama in the same sentence, and what do I get? A bunch of…" He looked to the other women to supply the answer and Eden wanted to yank their hair when they chorused, "Feminine drama."

Even Kellie looked like she was trying really hard not to laugh. And Eden wanted to rip Reid up and back down again, but instead she just shook her head and sat back down. He kept talking and he might have said important things about stress, but she didn't hear a single one of them. Feminine drama.

Then they followed Reid outside for a lesson on how to be a cowboy. Kellie sidled up next to her while the other women rushed to stand next to him. But he held the door open for them to go first.

Kellie slowed and said, "You know this is for Reid, right? The man's going crazy stuck here." Her eyes might have been asking for some sympathy on the man's behalf, but Eden couldn't help his clueless male-centric opinions.

But she stopped beside her. "I'll try to remember that."

"Hey, Eden, Kellie." Reid stood with the door open, waiting for them to come, presumably.

"It's okay, we'll be out in a sec." Kellie waved him on.

But he stayed put, stubbornly holding the door.

And with a huff, Eden grumbled. "Of all the…"

As soon as she walked through the door, Kellie right after, he winked. "Thank you. I feel like I'm being useful for someone when you let me do stuff like that." He stepped closer. "I'm going crazy here. Humor the cowboy? I'll make up for my mansplaining later?" He waited, and the twinkle in his eyes was almost her undoing. If it wasn't coupled with the tiniest hint of patronizing, she might have fallen all the way into being charmed. But she laughed. And that was enough for him apparently.

Eden made her way back to Kellie. "Is he always like this?"

"Like what?"

"Like…in control of everything?"

"Oh yeah, he's the chute boss." She laughed. "I mean, not really. Ryan is actually working on being the actual chute boss in the arena, but they all kind of defer to him sometimes." She nodded. "And he's never led them wrong." The pride she felt in all the guys, in Reid, was obvious. And it made Eden second-guess her rash irritation. But how else could it be interpreted? The man was insanely chauvinistic, wasn't he?

"The other guys take it?"

"Well, I don't know that they take it. They give it too. But they've worked out their ways of dealing with stuff. Look, Eden. You've seen him, the real him. He's a softie."

"Yeah, but not when I met him. I think maybe he's just a softie when he has a head injury."

"At least you saw what's on the inside early on."

"Hm." Eden wasn't so sure. She did appreciate Kellie's perspective though.

They gathered around Reid for whatever this next instruction would be. Reid picked up an ax and sliced through three logs with one swing of his powerful body. And Eden would have been a little dry in the mouth herself, had the other girls not been falling all over each other, giggling about his little demonstration.

Kellie smirked.

"Why are you watching me?"

"Oh, I don't know. I just get a kick out of you pretending to be so angry with him when right now, I know what you really want is to run a hand along that bicep." She laughed and walked away at Eden's open mouthed ready refusal.

But Reid pulled off his long sleeve shirt leaving only a more fitted t-shirt underneath and the definition on that man was not something to underestimate. Wow.

"Now let's have you try it." He glanced over at Kellie. "You sure about this?"

"Sure I'm sure."

But he still hesitated. "They don't need to be chopping their own wood."

Eden narrowed her eyes. "You saying we can't?"

"Not at all. But a man can do this so simply, why worry about it?"

Eden placed hands on her hips, ready to respond but Kellie stepped forward. "'Cause not all women plan to need a man for every little thing requiring muscles. It's okay, just show them."

"I think I got it." Eden stepped forward, holding out a hand for the ax.

Reid handed it over. "It's all in the swing. The momentum—"

"Thanks." She stretched her arms over her head one at a time, no need to pull a muscle. And then swung the ax around a couple times to get used to its weight and balance. By the time she swung it back and then down onto the log, she had enough force going that it split partway down the middle.

The other ladies clapped.

"That's good! Better than I expected. Now just lift the

whole thing together and bring it down onto the block. It should split the rest of the way."

Eden was irritated she hadn't split the log on the first try and now, the whole thing was so heavy, she didn't think she could manage. Which proved Reid's point about needing a strong man. She didn't mind admitting to fewer muscles. It was just the assumption that women could just grab the nearest man to do hard things. Many of these women would not have that luxury. She didn't. But luckily, she also had no need to split logs. Her first attempt to lift the whole thing showed that she'd need a little help. When her eyes caught Reid's, he jumped forward and wrapped his arms around her like he'd been waiting for just such an opportunity. And she admitted that being held by him was high on her list of anticipated moments in the day. She laughed. "Okay, now what?"

"Now, we'll lift together. It's the same as the initial split you attempted. But heavier."

She nodded.

Together they lifted the ax and log into the air and then, with the force of his arms behind her, they brought it all down together. The log split in two. "Mm. Let's do that again."

His gentle almost nuzzle of her ear sent a raging trail of goosebumps along her neck, and she could do nothing about the warmth on her face. But she tried to act unaffected. "Thanks for that help. I'd like to do it in one try sometime."

"We can work on that." He nodded. "I'll be out here any time." He looked up at the rest of them. "For anyone. If Kellie says it's important to chop your own wood, then we'll get you chopping your own wood." He shrugged like he couldn't understand such a thing, but he was a good sport about it. Eden decided she might have misunderstood his earlier comments.

When he'd helped every woman cut through a log, Kellie told everyone they were finished with the workshop. But Eden lifted the ax again and placed a log on the block.

Reid stepped back.

"I just want to do this." She swung the ax even though her arms quivered a little from the exertion. This time, she came down harder. The ax went into the wood, almost to the end and stuck.

"Dang."

"Nice. You almost had it. Let's get that one split and you can try again."

She nodded.

He helped her finish and then picked a smaller, lighter looking log on the block then stepped away.

This too, got stuck on her ax.

Three more and she still hadn't cut through a log in one try. And her arms now screamed in agony with every lift of the ax.

"Why don't we take a break?" Reid grinned.

But she waved him away. "I have to do this."

He studied her a minute then nodded.

But she tried three more, and it was obvious the task was getting more difficult rather than easier.

But before he could say anything more about a break she put the ax down. "I guess that's it for today."

"Why do you want to do this?" He shook his head.

"Look, Reid. I know that I don't need to know how to split a log. I don't have to be as strong as any man or anything, but when I swing the ax, when I see you send it through the wood like that? I want to feel that too. Sometimes, I just want to *feel* strong."

Something seemed to light his eyes then and he nodded. "Then we're gonna do this." He reached for another log.

"No, you don't have to manage this for me."

"I'm not managing it. Now come here. Let's give it another go."

"This isn't managing?"

He shook his head. But she let him, because leaving the job without finishing it was not sitting well with her either.

"So, it's all about the swing, the momentum in the ax, and where you hit it."

She watched him demonstrate a good place to hit the log. "I don't know about this. I think my arms might fall out of my shoulders."

He shook his head. "No. You got this. Once you start down this path, you gotta finish it."

She tried to push aside the coaching she was getting and take it just like that, good natured assistance, which she wanted.

"Here." He held out the ax and lifted another log onto the block.

Everyone else had gone back inside by now. Bear had come to join them from wherever on earth he had been exploring. Reid stood close. "This is important to you, right?"

She nodded.

"Okay. Then here we go. I have all night." He backed away and watched her closely, and somehow instead of the domineering man from earlier, this presence, this support, gave her strength. She stared at the log, gripped the handle of her ax and swung it back, bringing it high over her head and down onto the center of the log, right where Reid had shown her.

The cracking sound rang out through the air around them.

"Open your eyes."

She gasped, realizing they were squeezed tight. "Oh!" The log lay in two and her ax was deep into the cutting block. "I did it!" She clasped her hands together and turned to him.

"Yes you did." He tipped his hat to her. "This here is a cowboy salute." Then he winked. "Not sure why it's so important to do something you just send your man outside to do, but…"

She tried not to bristle. She knew he meant well, but a wave of irritation rose up inside. "Cutting wood isn't a man's job, really though, right? I mean, I'm happy to have it be anyone's job, but why a man's? Because you have to be strong? I feel strong. I feel like if I wanted this job, it should be my job."

He let out a long breath before he spoke, and she wondered what part of his cowboy code she'd offended. But all he said was, "I don't want my woman to have to come out here in the cold, to have to rub her hands raw with effort, to have to carry in a stack of wood, get splinters on her soft hands. It's a matter of pride that my woman won't have to do any of that. Because that's why she has me." He tipped his hat again and then he turned. "I'll be seeing you later, Eden Cooper."

"I want that too." The words came out before she could stop them.

He eyed her over his shoulder. "Then we just might get along."

She wasn't so sure about that. Because yes, she'd blurted out his fantasy sounded nice. But the reality was she didn't like sitting back, letting another do the work she could do.

That's why she'd enlisted. Someone had to do it. And she wasn't gonna sit back and shirk her duty. Did she not live in this free country? Did she not benefit from military protection? She'd better do her part. And as awful as it had been, as scarred as she felt, she had never been more proud of herself as she was while serving. She'd felt strong. Mighty. Useful. And important.

Chapter 15

Reid shook his head more times walking out across the property than he had in a long time. After a few minutes, her dang dog, Bear, came bounding up after him. "You stay over there where you belong."

The dog seemed to not carry one pang of remorse. He ran along at his side, as though he and Reid were friends or something. And if Eden loved this dog, Reid supposed it was his friend. But he carried no kind feelings for it.

Reid's head had stopped aching. He jumped around a little, moving from side to side. Nothing seemed to rattle. No dizzy spells overtook him. No pain. He was going back to the doctor the next morning and he didn't admit it to anyone who asked, but he was nervous. José had said he wasn't letting Reid back in the arena until the doctor cleared him, until he said he was not in danger of further injury. Well, that was plum ridiculous since bareback riding caused injuries all the time. But what could Reid do about it? Festering over what the doctor might say wouldn't do a dang thing, and he was done with the whole thing.

And he missed his trailer. And his horse.

He sure liked being this close to Eden though. He kicked at the dust in his path. Except for today. What on earth had gotten into that woman? She picked today to start unearthing the powerhouse DC woman? And she *was* a powerhouse DC woman, he reminded himself.

He grumbled for a moment about it. What was wrong with women these days? What was wrong with letting a man do his job? What was a man for if not to cut her wood, take out her trash, mend her fences and eat her food? He frowned. Of course some woman, somewhere was gonna find something wrong with what he just said. One of the things he liked about Lost Creek was that people just seemed reasonable about his thoughts on things.

But Eden had been so dang determined to split the stupid log. Fear? Grit? He couldn't pinpoint what motivated her but when the log finally split, he knew by looking at the joy on her face, he'd done the right thing by helping her. She talked about being strong. Well, he'd seen it, and she saw it in herself. And maybe that's all she needed. Maybe she needed a sense from him that she was strong? Like muscularly strong? He snorted. The woman was lean and lithe, a runner. And his first impression of her was that despite her size, she looked like one strong woman. But soft enough. He smiled. Could he get that woman back in his arms before too long? He hoped so. Not if he kept sending new fire to her eyes though.

Might be better when they weren't under the same roof.

He'd think more on it. 'Cause he had never felt so close to a woman. They were awesome together when they weren't setting off each other's buttons. He grinned. And she kissed like nobody else.

He kept walking. Sometimes walking made him smarter.

Not today, apparently. Today it just made the world more confusing.

His phone dinged.

The Chute. Nice.

Heeeey. He texted to the group. Then he scrolled up to see what he missed.

Oh. Look who's back. Eden must have dumped you. Eric.

Not too far off. I think she's triggered by me or something.

Triggered sounds like a good thing dude. Westin.

I thought so but I think it's more than just like…triggered…you know? Like I make her madder than that cat stuck in a barn last spring. Comes out clawing and hissing at you and you're just trying to save its sorry butt from starvation. He grinned at the memory. And the analogy wasn't too far off.

What you trying to help her with? Eric's grin was visible in his memory. And Reid had to laugh.

Normal stuff. The woman insisted she wanted to split a log.

Hey, some women are like that.

They made a whole bunch of jokes about strong women.

She's the one wearing the boots in that relationship. Eric chimed in and Reid had to concede he and Eden didn't really have a relationship. Then he said what was bothering him most.

But I don't know if I can be with a woman who won't let me help her… And that was the crux of it. He'd finally put into words what was needling at him. *We would drive each other crazy. And she'd be spitting and clawing at me when I least expect it.*

But are you helping her for her or for you?

The GIFs that followed Westin's question made him laugh. The wise old guy in glasses, the lady shrinks.

He finally had to come to the guys' rescue. *You're saying maybe there are ways I can help that I'm not thinking of? That she might appreciate more.*

A large bullseye emoji had him frowning again. He hoped it wasn't something like—go out there and actually put in time on her non-profit. He kicked at the dirt again. He knew of all the things, she might appreciate that gesture the most. But if he gave it some thought there might be other things as well. And at the moment, he had a rodeo to win. If he could actually ride in it. Bear whined next to him and went perfectly still. The only part of him moving was his nose, madly sniffing the air. Then the hairs on the back of his neck went up, and Reid knew he was in some kind of trouble.

He squinted in the direction Bear was looking. And then he froze too. The largest cat he'd seen outside of a zoo was creeping toward them. Not hiding, not racing, but steadily approaching, with body flat and head down. "Bear."

The dog growled.

And Reid should have been comforted by that. This mammoth of a dog could take that bobcat, couldn't he? Maybe. But it was Eden's dog. And she obviously loved it. But what was he to do about this?

"Easy, Bear."

The dog growled louder.

The cat was almost close enough to see the spots on its fur. And Reid was without ideas. He looked around. Nothing. No trees, no structures. No trucks. Just him and Bear. He stood taller and raised his hands in the air. "No!" He shouted. "Back!"

The cat paused, sunk lower on her paws and then started creeping forward again.

"No!" He jumped and shouted.

The cat kept moving. Then she veered to the right like she was thinking of circling them. "Oh, that's not good."

He stomped at her. "No!" He jerked, ran, and then bounced back. Nothing. She crept closer as she circled, and he began to feel what it was like to be stalked. Would she leap at them? Bear inched closer to him, and the two of them turned to face her as she circled. Now and then he shouted, but it seemed to have no effect.

And then everything seemed to happen at once.

A shout from far away caught his ear, the sound of a car or something giving him a tinge of relief. But the cat lunged, and Bear crouched, looking like he was going to take the hit head on. Eden's face flashed through his mind as Reid leapt in front of the dog, striking out with his boot. He connected with some part of the cat, and lost his balance.

The cat leapt up again, and Bear lunged for it. The two began a snarling rolling fight, the cat batting at Bear's face and Bear barking and biting at her neck.

A gun shot into the air sounded, and the cat startled and took off running.

Reid turned to see one of the more beautiful sights of his life. Eden with a shotgun raised, standing up on Kellie's ATV, watching the bobcat run away.

Bear leapt up to her, licking her all over her face.

Only then did she look away from the retreating cat and shower love on her dog. "You okay, big guy? Did that mean cat get you?"

After a minute, she turned to Reid who was just getting up off the dirt, dusting his pants. "Did I see you come between Bear and a bobcat?" Her face was shining, full of gratitude.

"For a minute. Then there was nothing more I could do. But Bear held his own. That's one tough dog."

"And you're one tough cowboy." She hopped down off the ATV.

"Should I be nervous you're still holding the gun?"

"Only if you want to be." She wrapped her free arm up and around his neck, tugging at him.

Happy to scoop her up, he lifted her and pulled her close. Their kiss was intense, if he had to put a label on it. She seemed determined to say something. He didn't know what. But it was coming on fiery and…angry? No, more like determined. And…strong. But he stopped analyzing things when she nipped at his lip with her teeth and slowed things down with a powerful intensity that stole every last thought. Suddenly, the only idea in his mind had something to do with her, and a rush of energy through him. "Mm." He pulled her closer. He explored her mouth, adjusting every angle, pulling her lips into his own, urging, asking, loving. Loving? It felt like love, or what he knew of love, cherishing this woman who challenged him and filled him at the same time. His arms tightened around her, one hand reaching for the gun, but she snatched it back.

"What if you drop it?" he mumbled against her mouth.

"You don't think I know how to be careful with a firearm?" Her eyebrow rose in challenge, and he remembered who he was talking to. "Right. Sorry." He covered her lips again before she could get truly offended by him. Perhaps he had a thing or two to learn about women. Certainly about this woman.

He carried her to the ATV and set her on the seat, pulled her close so her legs wrapped around his waist. But then Bear joined them and his licks on his face were not welcome. He growled. "Animal."

But when he turned to the large and drooly dog, sitting

way too close to Eden, she laughed and loved on her dog so much, he could only pet him too.

"He just wanted a kiss too."

"And that is something that will never happen."

Bear's enormous wet tongue slipped across his cheek.

"Ah!" He wiped at his face. "Control your animal."

"Oh stop. He's just being friendly. Besides he's gotta say thank you somehow."

Reid sighed. "I should probably thank him too, now that you mention it." He pet the dog's head again. "You're not so bad, Bear."

"As far as a thank you, that could use some work, but since it's only a dog, and he doesn't know better, I think I'll let it pass."

"We have you to thank the most. How did you know to come out here?"

"Honestly? I don't know. I was thinking about you and splitting the log and what you said about helping your woman." She laughed. "So I grabbed the gun and went for a drive."

"What? Really?"

"Sort of. I figured I'd do some target practice. It helps me think."

"Shall we?" He turned on the four-wheeler.

"Sure. I guess." She pointed. "I heard there are actual targets past those trees there."

"Right where the cat went?"

"Uh, right. Maybe we go that other direction?" She pointed over toward a ridge.

"Not into the rock. It could ricochet..." He stopped. "And I need to stop assuming you don't know things."

"Well, I don't know some things. I'm not a cowgirl. But guns I do know."

"Right. Let's go see who's the better shot."

Bear ran beside and Eden rode behind him with her arms wrapped around his back. And he thought that without too much effort, he could get used to this, real fast.

Chapter 16

Eden got ready for girls' karaoke night at the local bar, trying not to be disappointed that Reid couldn't come. Karaoke was great, right? And she'd really started to enjoy these women, or at least respect them and all they'd been through. But this was a big night for Reid, and she wanted to spend at least some of the night with him. Tomorrow the doctor would tell him if he was cleared to ride again. Eden knew he was worried about it. But girls' nights were important too.

Tracey peered in her bedroom door at Eden in her spot on the floor in front of the mirror. "You about ready, sunshine?" Tracey's long legs stretched out under a tight mini skirt. Her glitter tank would catch the karaoke lights. Her heels matched.

"Wow, you're gonna win whatever it is a woman gets for being the most fabulously dressed."

She laughed. "Or I'll just feel fantastic. You know I can't sing a single note, but I'm gonna look good doing it."

Eden stood. "There's something freeing about looking really great even when there's not a man in sight."

"Oh, they'll be in sight."

"What do you mean?"

"After girls' night, they come in to dance with whoever's left."

"What? You mean they like wait outside for us to be done?"

"Something like that. I'm just telling you what I heard. But you're right. Getting all dressed up just for me felt great."

Eden followed her out and down the hall. "I'm glad I got to know you, you know that? You deserve some real happiness."

She shook her head. "I know what you mean and thank you, but I think I'll be a lot happier if I don't think I deserve anything. If I work for it, great, if I'm surprised by it, great, but expecting something or feeling entitled to it has brought me nothing but disappointment." The hurt Eden knew ran deep shone for a second in her eyes. But she blinked it away. "But I know that's not what you meant. Sorry. When I'm used to doing therapy with someone it's hard to take the conversation light again, isn't it?"

"No need. I think I just learned a whole heck of a lot just now."

The others met outside the front door. When Kellie joined them, they climbed into a large white van. "You ladies ready to sing?" Kellie sat in the driver's seat.

"You know we are!" Tammi sat in the passenger seat. Apparently she'd been singing her whole life, and this night was the moment she'd been waiting for.

Eden laughed. "I'm ready if everyone promises not to judge."

"Same rules apply there, ladies. We are the safe spot for each other. I've reserved us a table up front. Drinks are on the ranch."

A little liquid courage would go a long way, but Eden wasn't going to drink tonight. She wanted to be there for Reid in the morning and something about facing the fear of singing in front of a group while completely sober felt exhilarating. Or insane.

"Tonight is a big night for Lost Creek, sort of a homecoming."

"What's going on?"

"Lots of the families are in town for the rodeo." Her eyes met Eden's in the rearview mirror. "The Original Six are all back together. And this rodeo is televised."

Would Reid be coming tonight? They hadn't talked about it. She smiled. They'd been too busy scaring away bobcats. And that kiss. She didn't know what to do with her growing feelings for Reid. She'd seen hints enough to know that the original assessment of Reid hadn't been too far off, at least the part about thinking he knew everything and women all over him. But the other sides to Reid, the soft caring side, the sensitive understanding side, the man who would cry with her over her pain. She would have never thought those sides to exist in Reid. She had to admit he was hot in every way, even the infuriating things about him, but would he ever be more than a three-week fling? How could they possibly make anything work between them?

She resisted texting him to ask if he would be there. Ladies' night at the bar was just that. For the ladies.

They arrived to a packed parking lot. "You weren't kidding. Looks like the whole county showed up." Tammi softly whistled.

"I told you. This weekend is a big deal." Again, Kellie's

eyes met Eden's. She decided to text Reid. *Thinking of you. Fingers crossed about the doctor.*

Thanks

That was it. But that small connection felt better. Apparently, a lot of people's hopes and expectations were riding on him being able to be at this rodeo. A town full of people cared. He cared. And Eden cared too. But she also knew how much trouble a concussion could be for the rest of his life. Was a rodeo worth a permanent head injury?

The women surrounded her, and they walked in together. Eden couldn't remember the last time she'd felt such strength from a group of women. "Let's do this!"

Roosters was packed with women. But Kellie pushed through the group, saying hi to nearly every person there, and showed them their table. As promised, it was dead center, right in front of the small stage, just perfect for a live band.

"Tonight is our night!" She held her hands in the air and several tables of ladies cheered for her.

Eden laughed. "Wow. Looks like drinks are already going round."

Their waitress showed up. Drinks, chips and salsa, and water for Eden were ordered. She sat back in her chair, listening and watching. Women wore every kind of outfit. Some were dressed like she always imagined rodeo women would dress. Turquoise. Boots. Frills on their shirts. Short denim skirts. Others wore more dance club-like attire. Some wore all black. And just about everyone there looked like they might have used half a can of aerosol hair spray to get their hair to stay put.

Women were there to have a good time. And Eden was determined to do just that.

A group of ladies from the next table joined them,

scooting their chairs closer. One was already walking a little unsteady and was louder than most.

Kellie steadied her. "Whoa there, Jess."

"Oh I'm fine, Kellie. This is just for one night. I'm back on the wagon tomorrow." She waved her away.

The concerned expression on Kellie's face told Eden this woman had no place to be drinking, but what more could they do?

A guy stood up front. "Welcome to the one, the only, the famous, Rooster's ladies night!"

The cheers made Eden smile.

"And now, let the karaoke begin!"

The first few girls got up there, and some of them were actually quite good. The cheers were loud and crazy no matter who sang or how good or bad.

Tracey and Tammi got up. Eden's whole table stood through their entire song. And they embraced the women when they returned.

This. Right here in this bar was how women were supposed to treat each other. Eden ran up to the stage to be next. She bit back her apologies for not knowing how to sing and just chose her song, "She's always a woman to me." By Billy Joel.

Everyone screamed in appreciation. And even when she sang her first note, they just started swaying together wherever they were, joining in. "She's always a woman to me." Eden laughed and sang some more. When she returned to her group with hugs from all and loud cheers all over the place, Kellie winked at her.

Eden didn't know if there could be any better therapy than this night right here.

And then Jess started moaning about there being no men in the room. "But Reid said he was coming."

At the name, Reid, Eden scooted a little closer to Jess, her ears straining to catch the woman's next words.

"Are you two still together?" someone asked.

"No way. Not after the way he treated me. That man is no good. I don't care what Kellie says about her Original Six. He's a player. And he did me wrooong."

"But he said he's coming?"

"Well, yeah. I still like to look at him." She took another long drink. "I don't think I'll ever get over that man." Tears started to flow. "But when you think you're gonna get married to someone.... We picked a ring. You don't get over them. Especially not when the month before, he's out romping in his truck with Steff, from Highpark."

Eden tried to give Reid the benefit of the doubt. The woman was obviously bitter and drinking like crazy. But *something* had broken her heart. *Something* had pushed her to drink. And it had Reid's name all over it. "And you know about that whole thing with Livvy. She's still taking care of their child."

Eden choked. "He has a child?" She couldn't stop the words even though she didn't want them spoken, didn't want the implications to be true.

Kellie shook her head. Which made her feel a little better.

Jess shrugged. "Probably not his, really. But Livvy was certain at first. The whole town talked about it."

"They did talk about it. But Jess, you know she came out later telling everyone whose baby it was."

"Probably I'm not remembering it right. Kellie would know."

Eden tried to make her heart return to normal. But her mind took her to the night of the gala. He had so comfortably left the room with six other women, two of them hanging on his arms. Who was Reid Browning, really? She'd seen so many different sides to him. So much she liked. But this side, his player side. She'd almost forgotten all those women and him so comfortably keeping them happy. She pressed her lips together. Maybe it would be good for him to head on back to the fairgrounds and his trailer. Living in the same house with the man was clouding her judgment.

She tried to forget what she just heard, but Jess would bring him up again throughout the night, and it jabbed at Eden's peace of mind every time.

All the women in their group had taken their turn singing. As well as a good third of the women in the bar. The night was drawing to a close. And then a man stood up at the front. "Ladies."

Everyone cheered.

He waited for the room to quiet somewhat. "We love Lost Creek!"

They cheered again.

"And now, as our ladies' night karaoke is about to end, I just wanted you to know that there is a parking lot full of cowboys out there banging down the doors to get in here with all of you. Do you have a dance or two for a rooster?"

The cheers turned deafening.

"Okay, okay. They know this night is all about you. So as always, you come tell me if any one of them isn't a gentleman."

And then the drums started. "And now. A special surprise. Pulled in from rodeos all over the country. Our one and only rodeo stars, from our own Sam Houston College, the Original Six: Ryan Prosper, Reid Browning, Westin Farr, Ford Hopkins, Eric Davis, and Lars Jackson." He shouted into the microphone.

The ladies got louder and louder, and when the first pair of boots walked out onto that stage, every woman was on her feet, screaming.

Eden was amazed at the energy, at the love and at the crazed fandom these boys carried here in Lost Creek.

The guys smiled and waved. And every one of them looked uncomfortable. But Reid pointed, and women right and left pretended to be caught by him.

Jess moaned. "I can't bear this." But she stayed right where she was, watching him.

And then when Eric took the microphone, she screamed with the rest of them.

"We feel a bit outnumbered." Eric's blush was charming. Eden knew these guys had good hearts.

The women screamed in answer.

"But we do have a song for you. Not all of us can sing like Ford here, but we're gonna do our best." The music to "Cowboy Dreaming" came on, and Eden didn't think it was possible, but everyone went even more crazy. The ladies, still on their feet, started swaying together. Tables of people linked to each other. Her group rushed to the stage, pushed forward by everyone behind them.

And Reid's eyes met Eden's. Despite herself, she reached for the hand he held out and before she knew what was happening, she was on stage in his arms. They danced, the women screamed, and the guys tried to sing.

She tried not to look at Jess.

But soon lots of other women had joined them on stage, and couples were dancing all over the place. They must have opened up the doors. The place felt twice as packed, which was saying something.

Reid pulled her closer. "How was your ladies' night?"

"It was awesome." She shouted into his ear.

He spun her in place. "You wanna get out of here?" His eyes pleaded. She knew he was worried about tomorrow, knew he needed to get to bed early, and she had some questions to ask him anyway. "Thank you!" A whole county full of people stood between them and the door to get out.

"I know the back way."

"Perfect."

He reached for her hand and led her back behind the stage, through a door to a lit hallway. "It's just me, Earl."

The man who had been at the mic waved from his office while they hurried to another door and then outside.

The night air felt pleasantly chilled after the heat of Roosters. He kept her hand, and they moved through the parking lot to his truck. "Let's go to a park."

"There's a park?"

"Sort of." He smiled.

He held her door and she climbed up into his truck.

They drove in silence for a minute before she braved disturbing the nice vibe between them. "So, I sat with Jess during karaoke."

At first his face was blank. "Jess?" He looked as if he didn't know who she was talking about.

"Yeah, she had a lot to say about you."

He frowned. "Is she from Lost Creek? Do I know her?"

"I don't know where she's from. Said you two dated, picked out rings."

He shook his head. "Doesn't ring a bell." Then he frowned. "Wait. Oh, no, now I know. The ring girl."

"Pardon?"

"The ring girl." He started to laugh but then stopped when she didn't look amused. "Look, no. Eden. I don't know what she said about me. She's been known to say a lot of things. But I'm about to tell you the truth. She and I went on *one* date. One. And it wasn't even a real date. We met at Roosters, danced a few, drank a few too many, and I asked her if she wanted to …" His face turned red.

"Go to the park?"

"Uh, yeah. Maybe we'll go someplace else." He turned his truck around.

"So that's it? One date?"

"That's it. She came to every rodeo after. She waited for me at the end. She even travelled with us a couple times."

"And you never dated her again."

He shook his head. "No way. She was a nightmare waiting to happen. She started talking about how we picked out rings, and she was expecting a proposal any day after following us around for a couple weeks."

"It looked like she maybe shouldn't have been drinking tonight."

"I don't know. All I know is that when I purposefully started bringing girls around for her to see, she spread the word that I broke her heart." Reid reached for her hand again. "I don't know what she said, or still says about me, but what I'm saying is the absolute truth. Ask any of the guys. Ask Kellie. She tried to explain to Jess how it all looked from her perspective, but Jess didn't listen. I think she believed only herself, talked herself into believing her own lies."

Eden thought the whole story incredibly sad. And even though it wasn't necessarily Reid's fault, it left sort of a negative light on everything. There was no denying his experience with women, that he was surrounded by lots of them who would dote on him, date him, hang out for the night. Did Eden really want to get caught up with a man who lived that kind of life?

The trouble was she thought she probably didn't, and

yet here she was driving with him to some other location to spend some more time together. She cared for him, was concerned about the results of his doctor's visit, had significant concussion experience and empathy. And … she admitted. Lived for his kisses, his manners, his cowboy charm. This man was oozing with so much of the stuff she loved in a man, but didn't think really existed anymore.

They pulled up to a water tower.

"Where are we?" She craned her neck and twisted to see out the front windshield.

"The view is amazing up there.'"

He dug in the back and handed her a large sweatshirt. "But can be chilly in the wind."

She hugged the shirt to her. "Thank you."

He circled around to get her door.

Was she really going to climb to the top of a water tower?

He led her to a hole in the fence and held it open for her to climb through.

Yes. She was. She laughed.

"What? Too sophisticated for these sorts of things?" His eyes held a challenge and though she was about to agree that yes, she had grown beyond high school water tower experiences, the challenge in his face made her hold her tongue, and he knew it would. His knowing grin told her as much.

Not too many metal ladder rungs later, she was caught up in the adventure of it as much as if she were in high school again. Laughing at herself, she called down over her shoulder. "And what if we get caught?"

"We won't."

Such a typical guy response.

"The sherriff gave me permission to climb this tower whenever I want for all time."

"That sounds like a story."

"I can tell you when we get to the top…"

Reid probably had more stories to tell than time to tell them. And Eden found herself, despite her better judgment, wanting to hear them all.

Chapter 17

Reid and Eden dangled their legs over the edge of the grated metal platform. The wind had picked up, but Eden looked comfortable in his sweatshirt. She looked more than comfortable. Seeing her in his clothes was doing things to him, and he fought the urge to scoot back and pull her into his arms.

They hadn't said much, and he wondered what went through her mind. That Jess woman had caused more problems for him than any man deserved. But he had heard she really did have a problem with alcohol. And she seemed lonely. So he kind of just let her be.

Eden rested her arms on the railing. "Lost Creek is a beautiful place."

"It really is. These small towns are such a classic slice of America. How many of our people are really living just like this, in their own small towns? No one really interviews them on television. No one knows how they feel about issues. They pretty much get zero press coverage, but they make up a huge part of our country."

She studied him. "That was a really insightful thought."

"And is this surprise I hear in your tone?"

"No, of course not, but I *liked* that thought. It would be good for the people I surround myself with every day to hear what you just said. The members of Congress, the lobbyists, everyone who feels so important all the time, to remember that America is this too." She spread her arm out over their view of Lost Creek's twinkling neighborhood lights.

"But obviously you're making a difference. You're working for more than just your town or your small family or life. It's impressive what you do, and the people you influence have power to make change."

She nodded. "That's what we say all the time. But seeing all this makes me wonder, makes me realize really, that what this country needs even more maybe are grass roots workers, people willing to work with the *one* person, one at a time, to make a change."

"Now *you're* sounding profound."

She turned to him. "What I do want to talk about is your head."

"Oh, my head." He tried not to feel his frustration rising. "I'm so tired of this head injury. If the doc doesn't tell me I can ride, I might just do it anyway."

"No. You can't do that."

He sat taller. "I can. And I just might. You don't know…"

"Seriously. I know what I'm talking about here."

"Okay. You know what you're talking about, but you don't know what I'm giving up."

"Oh, I think I do."

He almost argued but instead, seeing some emotion behind her words, he turned to face her more. "Tell me."

She seemed surprised but also pleased. And that's something he'd rather see on her face than the frustration, or irritation, he could bring to the surface just as easily. She seemed to collect her thoughts. "You might not feel dizzy or even pain anymore. But effects of concussions last a long time. We are working desperately for solutions, but from what we can see so far, there are lifetime effects from brain injuries."

"Did you bang your head really hard? Fall?"

"No, mine are from explosions, the sounds of them over and over. They have seen brain injuries now, after the fact. I hate the effects. I hate my brain fog. I used to be well spoken. Now I'm never certain I'll be able to hold a single train of thought long enough."

"You seem fine to me."

"That's great. But I've learned to adapt. I switch word choices. I pause. Sometimes I'm fine. But I cannot be up talking to a committee of the Senate or at a gala like you saw and stumble over my words or lose my train of thought. I don't like it that I can't remember things. Strings of numbers. It can be only five minutes later, and I forget the whole thing. And some of my memories are gone. From the past. As if they never happened." She sighed, and he could tell this conversation wasn't easy.

"I just tell you these things so you take this seriously. Under no circumstance are you to ride unless the doctor says there's no risk of injury."

He opened his mouth to refute that statement, but she held up her hand. "No head injury, concussion related."

The nod he started was interrupted. "You do know how much my head gets shaken around, right?" He pulled up his phone to find one of Eric's YouTube videos with him riding bareback.

"I've seen you." She shuddered at what seemed like a terrible strain on his body.

"You have?" The idea that she had looked him up made him all kinds of happy.

"Oh stop. Yes. I googled you."

"And you watched."

"Yes, and I watched."

"Did you see the belt buckle commercial?"

Her face turned dark red.

"Ha! You did! I knew that commercial would do me some good someday." His laugh felt deep and comfortable in his belly. Spending time with Eden was good for him. "I looked hot. I know." He sat up taller. "Okay, let's be honest. Eric looked hotter. He manages a tan better than I do." He stretched out his arms like he cared.

"Are you being serious right now?" Eden shook her head.

"Truth?"

She nodded "Yeah. How much do you care about your shirtless self in a belt buckle commercial?"

"Not at all." He nodded. "But I do care that you watched it." He leaned closer. "How many times?"

"Reid. I'm not…oh stop." She turned pleading eyes to him, but he shook his head. "How many times?"

"Five or six."

He tipped his head back and laughed. "This is the best news of this awful week." Then he scooted closer. "You know. These past two weeks should have been the worst of my life, but I'm gonna remember them as some of the best days. Getting to know you, learning about all you're overcoming, working through my own stuff. It's been good, Eden Cooper. Real good."

"For me too."

"How is your journal coming?"

"I think I'm almost finished with the whole part about Iraq."

"Really! That's incredible."

"Thank you. I do think it's a powerful exercise. It's amazing how much more my mind is at ease about things. It's not a perfect fix, but I think over time, this is going to make a big difference. And more memories I thought I had forgotten keep popping up. So I included those too. Feels kind of like my brain is dumping its information."

"And that's good, right?"

"Yeah, I think so." She stood.

"You ready to climb back down?"

"Maybe. I don't know. I feel like I need you to understand. Reid, I've devoted my life to this concussion stuff. We have a bill we're trying to push through Congress that proves what I'm telling you right now. You don't want to mess with your brain. There is not enough conclusive evidence for that doctor to go off of. Even if he clears you. Or if he's the least bit inconclusive, it's worth it to sit this one out."

He shook his head. "You don't know what you're asking."

"You don't know what you're risking."

She stared him down, but he refused to let what she was saying sink in. Bareback riders got hurt. That's what they did. He knew that going in. He wasn't trying to win any contests for most healthy human.

"Look, Eden. I appreciate—"

"No. Stop. No patronizing appreciation. Either you're hearing me or you're not."

"I'm hearing you, but just because I don't drop everything and follow your unsolicited and uneducated suggestion…"

"Hey, unsolicited I grant, but uneducated? I'm far more educated than you for sure."

"How do you even get off assuming something like that? Do you know anything at all about my educational background?"

"No, of course not."

"Well, you didn't google far enough. I have enough degrees to impress even you. Just because I don't use them…"

"I'm not talking about degrees. This doctor will have degrees, but you can't tell me a small town doc here in Lost Creek knows more about concussions and their effects than I do."

"Why wouldn't he?" Reid's arms crossed, and he knew he could be intimidating to some. He should have softened his stance, even sitting, but she was starting to get under his skin.

But she didn't back down one step. In fact, she moved closer.

"That thing you're doing with your feet and your arms and stuff. That is what men do when they know their intellect isn't keeping up. This right here tells me you're weak."

"That is the most ridiculous thing I've ever heard. You know what? I don't think this conversation is going anywhere good. Do you?"

"Not if you stubbornly refuse to listen to reason and take care of your brain. It's the only thing you're gonna hope you have left when everything else stops working."

"I think there are more than enough people talking to me about my head. I don't need one more." He held his hand for her to start walking, but she refused to move.

"Are we finished up here?"

"You're free to go."

"I need to walk you down. I'd like to go first with you right above just in case anything happens…"

She shook her head in disbelief. "Look, I appreciate your constant attention and your desire to keep me safe and all that. But I've climbed things like this under the potential of enemy fire. I've scooted through desert sand. I've seen people blown…" Her voice cracked. "Blown apart right in front of my eyes. The children." Her face crumpled but she waved away his immediate steps towards her. "So I don't really need you keeping me from falling, thank you." She turned away.

When he didn't move for a long time, and neither did she, he gently called over to her. "I'm also your ride home."

Her huff would have been funny except he knew she wasn't amused. She was flaming mad and it was all his fault. "I'm sorry."

She shook her head.

"I'm real sorry."

"And that's just gonna fix things?"

"What's broken here? You are telling me to be careful just like everyone else. I am being careful. There's nothing more to talk about."

Her breath came out in a sigh of defeat. "I guess you're right. Yeah. Okay, let's go."

And right then Reid discovered that as much as her fight got under his skin, he liked her defeat least of all.

But they climbed down the water tower in silence.

The ride back to Kellie's was also quiet. He ended up turning on the radio to detract from the lack of conversation, something he'd never had to do with her before.

As soon as the truck stopped, she hopped down and ran into the house.

His head fell forward onto his steering wheel, and he sat still for many minutes, thinking about the disaster of an evening with Eden. And worse even than the train wreck he'd caused, he wasn't sure how to fix it. He wasn't sure that it was possible to fix.

Chapter 18

Eden woke the next morning later than she'd planned. She heard Reid's truck door shut. So she threw off the covers and raced to the front porch in time to see his truck at the end of the driveway.

Kellie joined her.

"How was he?"

"Silent."

Eden nodded.

"Heard you come in."

She didn't say anything for a long five breaths and then shook her head. "We don't really get along."

Kellie laughed.

"He pretty much hates me."

She laughed harder.

"And it's like I can't even have a conversation without trying to remind him he's not the boss of me."

"Well now, he should be used to that much at least." Her eyes twinkled.

"I just don't think he should be riding so soon after a concussion, no matter what the doctor says."

"And that, Eden Cooper, is a losing battle."

"So I learned."

Kellie turned to sit on the porch swing. "Sit with me."

Eden sat at her side, pulling her legs up to her chest.

"How are you feeling about your stay? Separate from Reid. I don't want whatever you two like to fight about to interfere with some actual healing."

"I'm good." She told her about the journal. "I really feel like some of that stuff I've been carrying inside is not haunting me anymore. It's in a different place or something."

"That's good. I think this week we can come up with some options to help with your memory and stress about speaking and things."

"Do you think there is more we can do there?"

"I think so. I've been looking into memory specialists and things. It's not my area, but I've found a couple good suggested ideas. And we can move from there."

"I'd love to try it." She rested a hand on Kellie's shoulder. "This has been worth my time in every way. Thank you."

She nodded. "I hope so. You know, you've given us some of you, too."

"Have I?"

"Certainly. Each of the ladies has learned from you, like you them. And you've been a real friend to me. No matter what that crazy Reid man does, I will always count you as a friend."

"Thank you. That means so much to me." Her eyes teared. "I'd like to still call or text or something when I get back to DC. If you aren't too busy."

"I'd like that. I don't usually maintain personal relationships with clients. Mostly because I want them to move forward, not cling backward. But you're different. You're a friend besides. And I just don't think Reid is gonna be letting go of you anytime soon."

Eden snorted. "I don't know if he can stand to hold on."

"You just don't even realize what kind of hold you have on that man. Why did he get so angry about you telling him to skip the rodeo?"

Eden shrugged.

"I'll tell you why. Because he knew he was gonna have to listen to you."

Eden's heart leapt with hope. "Do you really think he'll listen?"

"This first rodeo back?" She shook her head. "No. He'll go all out. He'll do what it takes. But he's doing it for the town. You saw at karaoke. This is important to the folks here. Rodeo put us on the map, built up the college, gave some of these people jobs. And hope and a life. He's doing it for them."

Eden considered Kellie's words, and yet couldn't feel comfortable with Reid riding no matter what his reason, but she also couldn't help but feel a new admiration for him. Reid surprised her at every turn.

Kellie stood. "And now, breakfast. Unless you're going back to bed."

"I know I'm dressed like it, but I think I'll get up and help you with the eggs."

"Now that's what I'm talking about."

Eden changed quickly and then joined Kellie in the kitchen with an apron tied behind her back.

She went through the motions of their day, but really

didn't feel or hear anything. Her mind was totally focused on the pending sound of Reid's truck coming down the drive, but it never did. Night fell, and she hadn't heard a word and she didn't see his truck. When she could wait no longer, she found Kellie in her room. "Hey."

"Haven't heard from Reid?"

She shook her head.

"I haven't either. But I'm assuming he's at the trailer. I could text the guys to see if they've heard anything." Kellie pulled out her phone and held it to her ear. "I'll just call Ry."

After a minute, she said, "Hey. We're wondering about Reid. No. He's not back here." The pause was too long. Eden wished so bad she was on speaker phone. "Okay. Thanks. Let us know if you hear anything."

Kellie dropped the phone on her bed. "They don't know. They assumed he'd be coming back here. Ryan doesn't sleep over at the fairgrounds. But he's gonna track him down."

Eden nodded. "Wow. He's…He's probably just thinking through some things."

"Yeah. He's a strong man, Eden. He can take a lot of what life throws at people. Maybe he just needs a minute."

And probably a minute away from her. She'd thrown such a fuss about her own opinions, and been so irritated when he didn't seem like he would be following any of them, he probably didn't want to have it out with her again, especially if he'd just received bad news.

"I just really ache for him, you know? It's hard to have an injury mess with your dreams, and…" She clenched her fists together. She didn't need to be crying to Kellie about this, but it was too late. The first tear fell. "And it's my fault. My dog gave him the concussion." She shook her head. "I'm gonna have to add him to my book."

"That's not a bad idea."

"You think I'm gonna have trouble getting over my guilt for this?"

"Maybe. Or just figuring out what you feel for the man. 'Cause whatever it is, it's strong. It's coming out your ears sometimes. Whether it's anger or attraction I can't tell, but there's an interest there that no one would deny."

Eden didn't want to talk about things anymore, so she mumbled thanks and left Kellie's room. Her feet took her out to the porch, and Bear leaned up against her. "Where you been, boy? You chasing any more bobcats?"

Her looked up in her face and leaned closer.

Rubbing his head, his back, she made her way over to one of the hammock chairs.

She lifted the phone to her ear, calling Reid for the second time that day. He didn't answer, but this time she decided to leave a message.

"Hey, Reid. Thinking about you. Wanna talk?" When she hung up, she knew there was so much more to say. But that's all she could bring herself to say over voicemail.

Sleep did not come easily that night. She worried and festered over Reid for an hour or more before she finally dozed, and then her dreams were riddled with Iraq, karaoke and Reid. And nothing made sense. After waking the second time to scared children at the Rooster, she got out of bed, even though it was nowhere near time to be up, and made her way to the kitchen for something, anything to distract her.

"Hey." Reid's form stepped out of the shadows, and Eden jumped.

"What!"

He lowered himself in the kitchen chair. "Sorry I startled you."

"No, it's okay." She stepped closer but then stopped. "Are you okay?"

"Yeah. I'm good."

He didn't look good. He shoulders were slumped, his face drawn.

"I'm warming some milk. Want hot chocolate?"

"Sure."

She started the burner and poured in milk. Then got out ingredients to make her special blend.

"What you got there?"

"Secret family recipe."

"And now I'm really looking forward to this." His words were fun. He was making an effort, but everything sounded a bit flat.

She worked in silence, feeling his gaze on her back. She was well aware of her short shorts, her tank, her unkempt hair, but what could she do about it? At least the room was dimly lit.

When she brought over his warmed cup and sat beside him, she wasn't certain he'd even be awake, but he nodded and brought it to his lips.

"Mm. This is good." He downed some more. "And the perfect temperature."

She smiled. And waited. What was the news? She was dying to know. But since she'd dumped so strong of an opinion on him, she didn't feel like she had a right to be in on his business at this phase.

"I'm riding."

"Okay."

He stood. "Well, I think I'll be sleeping in my trailer now that I'm riding." He eyed her.

But she had nothing to say.

"That's all you got?"

"What do you want me to say?"

"After all your harping on me for riding and not riding and everything, you got nothing more to say?"

"Well, I think I said it all, the word you used, 'harping' about covers it I think." She tried to blink back the hurt.

He took a half step toward her and then ran a hand through his hair. "Oh, come here. I'm sorry." He tugged her close and wrapped his strong arms around her.

She melted into him, loving the feeling, as well as hating him for being so obtuse. What was going on? What did the doctor say? Was he going against medical advice?

But he said no more. When he stepped back, he kissed her cheek and then slipped out the back kitchen door. And he was gone.

Something about it felt more final than any other time. Maybe because he wasn't sleeping here, maybe because she was going home in a week. Maybe because he was tired of her.

She made her way back to her room but instead of going to sleep, turned on the lamp by her bed and pulled out her journal.

Chapter 19

Reid heard nothing and saw nothing of Eden over the next three days while he tried to get his rusty self back on a horse and ready to compete. He kept his expectations low. Bare minimum he didn't want to embarrass himself. It was much better to hear an announcer say, "Wow, even after a two week break, he's still at the top of his game," than an excuse ridden explanation for just plain bad riding.

But his first time up in practice was nothing short of disastrous. And now, while he waited for them to get another horse ready, his head ached. And he knew it was from the injury. Eden's words echoed in his head. Did he wait till the next rodeo? Was he riding too early?

No. He had to shut out all her complaints from him head. He was in. He'd told José. He'd set up his boundaries. Reid was gonna ride. He'd just have to get used to the pain.

But the second time up, he was feeling dizzy. Not enough to wobble, but enough for his world to shake for a second.

Because of that, he told José no more for the day.

"That's right. Take it easy," José called to him as Reid walked away. The day was almost night anyway.

Not really paying attention to where he was walking, he almost ran into the guys.

Eric held out an arm. "Hey, you seeing us?"

"Now I am, not sure how a man could miss a bunch of lugs your size."

They smiled, every one, but there was that attempt to be sensitive thing going on and Reid was having none of it. "You guys here to wallow in my self-pity for me?"

Eric opened his mouth but then closed it.

"'Cause I've been going through the books and your scores are worse than what we were losing with at Sam Houston."

"They are not..." Westin began, but then he nodded. "Yeah. Just coming here for some pointers."

"That's what I thought. I think we could all use some pointers about now."

"Or a good cow tipping." Eric shrugged.

Reid snorted. "I thought we established that's not even a thing."

"It's a thing, but what we established is it's not a good thing."

"Oh right." Reid was about ready to call it a night. But Ford pulled out his guitar. And the others pulled out chairs. And the fire was lit. And someone brought out some drinks. And so instead of heading to his trailer, Reid plopped down in a chair.

"Remember when we first met?" Eric fiddled with a piece of straw then stuck it in his mouth.

"I do." Lars nodded. "We'd all come because of their much-advertised rodeo program. But come to find out..."

"We were it." Ford laughed. "Yep. That was a bit of a surprise."

"But we had Coach." Reid thought back to the man who'd trained them all, introduced them to the world of collegiate rodeo. Hank Woods. The guy could have ridden a bull with his eyes closed. And he had a finger of understanding on every event. Their group of six worshipped the man. And when he passed, they each struggled in their own ways. "And he's the reason I came to Sam Houston in the first place."

They all nodded. "And for the scholarships."

"True." Reid winced. "My dad wasn't gonna put one dollar into Sam Houston himself. It's a good thing rodeo pays, and I did get a little scholarship too."

"We spent every waking second trying to qualify for whatever rodeo would take us."

They were all quiet for a minute, Ford strumming different chords on his guitar. It felt nice, like so many moments they'd had together.

Suddenly Reid had to talk to them about Eden. "I took Eden up to the water tower."

Lars almost spit out his drink. "Did you do our chant?"

"Nah. She'd have thought I was dumber than she already thinks."

Ryan shook his head. "I'm sure she doesn't think you're dumb."

"You should hear some of the things she says, but that's beside the point. Being up there, even without you guys, made me remember."

"Yeah." Ryan kicked his toe in the dirt. "That didn't work out so well for me, did it?" His eyes met Reid's and like a punch in the gut, Reid realized he wasn't the only one in the world suffering from a life without rodeo, potentially.

"Promising we would rodeo till we die was a great thing for our college days when everything was pulling us in different directions, when everyone was telling us rodeo was a losing direction, there weren't no money in it. There was no future. We'd be destroying our bodies before our prime. Back then, saying give me rodeo or give me death meant something important. Who here regrets sticking it out?"

Not a hand went up.

"But now, dude. Now we got other things to consider."

Reid pointed to Ryan. "And we need you around, Bull-dogger. Look what you did, pulling us all together for this. The whole town is in on it. You gotta admit, that riding or no, it's cool to be a part of all this."

Every one of them nodded. And Reid didn't feel like he could say a darn thing about possibly having to step out, not with Ryan right there, knowing the man would never ride bulls again even though he'd loved it as much as Reid loved bare.

But Reid was hurting. The doctor gave his clearance, but his warning was also clear. Reid was at risk. A bad fall, a rough ride, if Reid felt any symptoms return, he was to take another break. All of it made his stomach sour, and he hadn't been comfortable since the appointment.

"Remember Reid's first ride bare?" Westin laughed.

"Hey, come on. That was my first ever ride."

"You were walking around holding your tenders for a week."

"Really not something we need to be remembering." He looked around, making sure no one else was listening in. Everyone had gone down, apparently. The place was quiet except for their little fire. And his closest friends.

"Look, guys. I know you're trying to make me laugh.

And I need this. Man I need this. I don't know how you do it, Ryan. I think if I lost rodeo, I'd be half a man."

Ryan's eyes looked pained, but there was a peace Reid hadn't really paid attention to. "I hear what you're saying and maybe you feel like you have no room to complain. But fact is, rodeo isn't gonna last forever for any of us. Just 'cause I went out first, doesn't mean we aren't all gonna be facing this same situation one day. How many old guys do you know getting knocked around on a horse?" He kept his voice light, but the words sunk in. "You're not out yet. I was watching you today. You're just riding timid. You're afraid of the voice in your head telling you not to get hurt."

"It's Eden's voice in my head."

"Well, now a woman's great for a lot of things. But riding rodeo ain't one of them. What woman doesn't sit there worrying her man is gonna get hurt while riding?"

Reid nodded.

Ford stopped tuning the guitar. "So, you think about Eden all you like before and after you bite the dust, but while you're on that horse, there's nothing there but the beauty of the moment. You got me?" Ford was making some real sense.

"I got you." Reid nodded. "You guys don't think I'm out yet?"

"No way. You got so much fire inside you. You're gonna be just fine. You been riding this whole time and never getting a concussion once, then you suddenly get knocked over by a dog?" He laughed and then lifted his cup to him. "If bareback ain't killed you yet, it's not going to."

The others agreed.

The relief that filled Reid could not really be described. But he sat back, looking on each of his friends, knowing things were gonna be all right.

"And you might want to talk to Eden, too. Kellie says she's like half a woman over there."

Reid leaned forward. "What is it with you guys and Kellie and Eden Cooper? It's like from day one everyone was pushing me toward her or something. Do you not know how infuriating that woman can be?"

The smiles on their faces were all different shades of sneaky, and he wasn't liking it one bit. "What is this?"

But not a word left their lips.

"You guys trying to pull some match-up?" He shook his head. "'Cause I know. For certain. That not one of you sorry saps is qualified to set me up with any woman." He paused at Ryan. "'Cept maybe you, as you've proven capable yourself."

They laughed even harder.

He frowned until Ford shook his head. "We aren't trying to set you up with anyone. It's just obvious you two are good together."

"I don't know what you're seeing, 'cause all I'm seeing is a fiery woman fighting back against everything I try to do or say."

"Everything?" Eric winked.

"Well not everything. She's fiery in good ways too." He grinned. He couldn't help himself. "But I'm sticking to our code. You're not hearing anything else about that from me." They were gentlemen about their ladies, to them, about them, with them, all of it. And he was proud of each one of his friends.

"Whatever you think we're doing, it's all in that messed up head of yours."

Reid kicked at the dirt. "You think I should call her?"

"Yes, man. Call the woman." Ryan nodded toward his phone.

"Okay. As soon as we're done here."

The guys all stood.

"Well, all right then." He waved them off. And he couldn't help but love his brothers— brothers in rodeo. They knew just what he needed tonight. And they were there for him.

The phone rang three times when he called her number, and he thought for sure it was going to voicemail but then a quiet voice answered, "Hello?"

"Eden?"

"Yeah, it's me."

Just hearing her voice set some things right in his mind. "I know you're right. But I just can't give it up. Sometimes a person has to do things just 'cause it's in him and he would die if he quit right now. But it doesn't mean I don't care. I just need to get you out of my head while I do crazy things so I can risk even harder things and win. Though I'm certain you are not happy to hear that right now." He winced, and waited. He knew he sounded like a dufus.

But her sigh was resigned. "I know. Do what you need to do."

"That's it?"

"Yeah. Sometimes when the steam wears off, I realize I can't change what's not mine to change."

"Hm." He headed for his trailer. "But I do listen to you. And I have found ways to change. Letting you cut your own logs, and all that." Wow, he was like a puppy Bear, begging for a little approval from the woman.

But she laughed. "Reid. Just go do your rodeo. Let's talk after."

"You coming?"

"Yeah, I'll be there."

Happiness surged through him. "Okay great. See you

then." Before he hung up, he said, "Wait. There are friends and family tickets waiting at will call. Better seats." And he would know right where she was sitting.

"Kellie told me about them."

"But use mine."

"Aren't they all together?" She stopped. "Okay. I will."

"And yes, they are all together." But it was important to him that he had a girl at the rodeo. And if she didn't understand that, so be it. He'd show her later. Plus, none of the ladies knew the little extras he'd planned.

"Good night, Reid."

"Good night."

The guys were right. He could put her out of his mind. She even sort of agreed to that. Ride bare and then see her after. Something about that felt as freeing as it did reckless. And now that the whole weight of his health and winning and somehow figuring out his seat on a horse fell on his own shoulders and no one else's, he recognized that the risks were perhaps as great as everyone said. But he was still getting up on that horse tomorrow. And he was gonna ride better than he ever had.

Chapter 20

Eden pulled up in front of the rodeo arena with all the other women from the ranch. Everyone had lengthened their stays so they finished the full three weeks together. She couldn't believe she would be going back home in a few short days.

Work had been piling up. Momentum was building for the bill she'd helped write, and it was about to be introduced on the House floor. She was pleased it had done so well in committee. She spent more and more time in the evenings catching up on emails, and she could feel her heart being pulled back into the work that held her passion.

Things with Reid were just so unspoken. She had no idea where she stood with him, no idea what she felt about him really. Except like Kellie mentioned. Whatever it was, the feelings were strong. What could they do moving forward? She had months of work ahead of her. He was sticking with rodeo, had just purchased land here in Texas. They seemed to be able to get along well enough when they weren't arguing over something. Perhaps it would be best to just let the relationship drift away when she left. So many questions, so many what ifs, ran through her mind.

But tonight was the rodeo. Kellie and the ladies entered together with all the crowds she had seen at women's karaoke. Families too. Everyone piling in with the ready excitement she was beginning to feel.

"The guys got us VIP seats this time." Kellie met her eyes. "Someone pulled some strings."

Eden smiled. Was that what Reid had meant, make sure to get his seats? "That's great." She followed Kellie, who grabbed the tickets from will call. The arena was circled by animal pens, stands that sold food, and hordes of people. "Wow, these things are really well attended."

"Oh yeah. This is Lost Creek's football game. We come together for our boys. These guys put us on the map." Kellie led them down the stairs, past row after row to the very front. "And here we are, compliments of you know who." She squeezed Eden in a quick hug and then fell in behind her. The other ladies joined. The lights dimmed and then strobe lights flashed, spotlights moved through the crowd and music played. A woman rode out on a horse, as fast as Eden had seen a horse ride in an arena. They came tearing around along the side and back out the back end. "Wow!" She leaned forward.

Then a man came prancing out on a horse. He had a microphone. "Good evening ladies and gentlemen."

The crowd went crazy.

"It is time for the one, the only, Lost Creek Rodeo, grand entry!"

All the lights went back on, and what looked like a parade began. A horse-drawn carriage came out first. The horses were decorated and marched in unison. People waved from inside the carriage.

Then a group of clowns came out, some on bicycles, some on foot. They ran and squirted water into the audience, then one with a large blue eye and a huge smile painted on his face, handed Eden a carnation.

She waved to them all as they ran by. Then the announcer quieted the crowd. "And now we would like to introduce our contenders, Lost Creek's own, the very first rodeo team from Sam Houston College, affectionately known to us as the Original Six!"

Six guys came flying out on horses. They were strong, their arms thick, and their bodies solid. They rode as though it were the most natural thing in the world to be riding on the back of a galloping horse. She spotted Reid right away. He wore all white. A white shirt with frills, white pants, a white hat. Silver studs lined his hat and his shirt. He tore out across the arena, circled around so that he was coming towards them, slowed until he was right in front of Eden, tipped his hat and then raced back to line up with the other five.

She'd never been singled out like that before. He was as handsome as she'd ever seen him. And something about knowing he cared for her, more than anyone in that arena, sent her stomach flipping around in a happy dance. She realized right then and there that she could never think anyone was as cool as Reid, riding in on his horse. She grinned.

The announcer called out, "And now, for anyone who doesn't already know these guys, Ryan Prosper." His horse stepped forward and bent one knee like a bow. Everyone laughed.

"Reid Browning." His horse danced in place.

"Westin Farr." His horse turned all the way around and showed its backside.

The crowd laughed.

"Ford Hopkins." Both front legs went in the air.

"Eric Davis." He turned sideways with his horse and the animal did almost a two-step towards them.

"And Lars Jackson." He waved and then he and his horse dipped their heads in unison.

The crowd went crazy.

The announcer went through all the other acts and fun events, including the rodeo queen who rode out and circled them all. She was dressed in pink with turquoise cowgirl boots and suddenly all Eden wanted in life was a pair of turquoise cowgirl boots.

"And now, if you would, honor our flag by rising with me as we hear 'The Star-Spangled Banner.'"

Everyone stood and the whole arena became quiet. Men took off their hats. Hands went over hearts. A huge flag unfurled by the scoreboard. Then two horses ran out, one trailing a US flag behind and the other a Texas flag.

Somewhere in the arena, the voice of a young girl sang out loud and clear, the words to "The Star-Spangled Banner."

Eden was carried away. Her hand cupped over her heart as she thought of her friends lost in defense of that flag, of freedom. She thought of her sight of it, flying at her barracks, remembered feeling inspired, strengthened by it, thinking that there were Americans on the other side of the ocean honoring the same flag, praying, hoping for freedom, caring for her. And here was evidence of that faith she had in America. Here in this rodeo arena people honored the flag just as she hoped they had.

When the song died down, everyone cheered again.

The announcer finally got everyone's attention. "You may all be seated. And now, we have the special opportunity to honor those in our audience who have served in the military. When you hear your song, if you are a military veteran, please stand."

Eden's heart pounded. Moments like this were important. She knew it. She'd dreamed of them over the years. But for some reason, standing in front of everyone during the army song was always difficult.

"I'll stand with you." Kellie's whispered assurance filled her with relief, and she squeezed her arm.

"Thank you."

True to form they played the army song first, and Eden stood with Kellie at her side as it started. What she didn't expect was Reid, who rode out across the arena carrying something. When he got close enough, she saw it was a small flag in a decorative case. "We honor our military here, Ms. Cooper. Thank you for your service." He bowed his head. The horse bowed and then he handed her the flag.

Tears filled her eyes. "Thank you."

"I can't believe I presumed to tell a war vet how to handle a gun."

Then she laughed. "It's bound to happen."

"I wanted you to know we made some donations." He pointed to a patch on his shoulder.

She looked closer. "Is that…?"

"The logo to Vets 4 Life? Yes it is. We are each riding for vets today. And I'm riding for one very special vet." He winked and returned to his line.

A tear traveled down her cheek but she ignored it, so full of emotion and even joy, that she didn't know what to say.

As they played the other songs, other vets received similar gifts until all the songs had been played and everyone was again seated. But she knew that a part of her would never be the same. She was so touched, so honored, so hopeful. "What a nice thing to do."

Kellie smiled.

Eden studied her flag. It was folded into a triangle and encased in glass with gorgeous wood framing. On the back was engraved, "To my favorite vet. Reid."

She fingered the words. This was all so thoughtful. How could she leave this man and go back to Virginia? Then she shook her head. How could she stay? Her vision blurred again.

"You okay, honey?" Kellie rested her hand across Eden's shoulders in a gentle squeeze.

"I think so."

The announcer continued. "And now, the moment you've all been waiting for, Lost Creek's own rodeo."

He went through each event, talking about each of the competitors and their past times. Eden loved every bit of every mention of Reid. She was fascinated by the whole thing, beginning to end. And she clutched the flag in her lap as though it were a treasure. And it was. No one had ever done anything like that before. She knew she'd be picking it up again to study it many years from now.

"He really is the most thoughtful person," she said to Kellie before she realized that the words would seem as though they came out of nowhere.

"I'm glad you can see it. He's as thoughtful as they come."

"I used to think rodeo was mean to the animals."

Kellie shook her head. "Those creatures are the bread and butter around here, treated better than just about anyone. This is the way it's done on the real working farms. All of rodeo is like that. It's a celebration of the cowboy way of life." Kellie's eyes filled with pride. And Eden was glad for the perspective.

There were no paper programs to read so she had no way of knowing what was coming first. But Kellie explained what events were called and what to watch for. After what seemed like every other possible thing had happened besides the actual competitions, Kellie nudged Eden. "Bareback is next."

And then every part of Eden's body tensed up. All the fear and stress about Reid riding came roaring back to life, and she clenched her hands together as if doing so would help him be safe.

Kellie pointed to the chute. "They've got Ryan in there as the chute boss right now. That's good. Reid trusts him."

Eden nodded, unable to form words. Her throat felt dry enough for a desert competition and the heart pounding in her ears had her gripping the railing.

The announcer called out someone's name; all Eden knew was it was not Reid. Then the words, "Reid Browning" had her on her feet, gulping back her fear.

Chapter 21

Reid heard his name. His horse seemed to know his time to go crazy had come. They'd used Spitfire today, and he was ticked. Reid's legs were stretched out in front of him. He gripped the railing at his side while he balanced himself. One hand secured the rope. His mind cleared, except for a dogged determination to ride good, ride hard, stay on for eight seconds, and be done with this. For today. "Eight seconds."

Ryan nodded.

But just as Ryan tightened the cinch on the already ticked off Spitfire, and the door opened, Reid's vision clouded.

Blinking furiously, shaking his head to try to clear things, he gripped his ropes but felt the world closing in darker and more invisible, crashing in around him until he saw no more.

When bright lights made his eyelids glow orange, sounds started to register. He tried to speak. "Did I stay on?"

"Wait. He's saying something." Someone's voice. A woman.

"Hush, y'all." Kellie sounded more concerned than he would have thought. "Say it again, hon. We didn't hear you."

His lids were too heavy. He couldn't open his eyes. But he tried to speak. "Did I stay on?"

The silence in response concerned him. He blinked and concentrated and at last his eyes opened, but only for a second. The light sent a searing pain straight to the back of his head. "Ouch."

"Good. I hope it hurts. I hope it hurts like hell." Eden. And she was madder than Spitfire apparently.

"Eden." Kellie's placating tone made even him cringe. He was sure Eden was about to lose it.

"No, seriously. *Did I stay on*? That's what he wants to know? How about did I die? Is my brain okay? Am I going to have concussion side effects for the rest of my life? Can I count to ten? The man can't even open his eyes." Her voice cracked at the end and Reid's heart ached for her.

"He's just being Reid. Can't blame the guy for wanting to win." Ah, the voice of reason. Maybe Eric? But he was asking for something fierce if he was gonna cross Eden right now.

"Yes, I blame him. And I told him. I don't even believe the doctor okayed this. What doctor in his right mind would have agreed to something like this, in his condition?"

"I was in my right mind, miss. Hello. I'm Doctor Larsen. Now, if I could get all overwrought people out of the room, I'd like to do an examination."

He tried to whistle. That wasn't gonna sit well with Eden.

But he heard nothing else. In fact, the silence in the room felt unnerving. "I can't open my eyes."

The light dimmed and he tried a peek. "Better."

Doctor Larsen leaned over his face. "Good to see you, Reid. Let's take a look and see what we can find, shall we?"

He tried to nod, but it hurt so he just said, "Mm. Hm."

"You in pain?"

"Yeah."

"At rest?"

"Dull."

"But if you move?"

"Yeah, sharp."

"So, I saw the video tape. You exited the chute, held on for about three seconds but started to slide sideways and then you went limp and dropped off the horse."

Reid groaned.

"So, no, you didn't last the full eight seconds. And it was alarming to see. If I wasn't looking at you now, I'd have thought you'd had a stroke. The horse nearly kicked you in the head. You can thank the clowns for your life when you get a minute."

He groaned again.

"And that woman, your lady maybe? She's in the waiting room, pacing like one of your barebacks in their stall."

Waiting room? "Hospital?"

"Yep, afraid so. You slept through the whole thing, but we got you here safe and sound and that's what's important. Now, can you open your eyes to focus on me for a minute?"

He did whatever the doctor said while his eye tracking was checked and his pupils and the feeling in his toes.

"We're gonna run a CT scan and keep you on all the monitors for a few days."

"Hmm."

"I'll be in and out of course, but I'm also calling in a concussion specialist your girl recommended. I checked, and he's one of the most highly recommended doctors in the country right now for concussion. She called in a favor, I think. You should meet him tomorrow as well."

"Thanks."

"You're welcome. I stand by my diagnosis. You should have been fine to ride. We'll figure out why the dizzy spell hit. It could have been something as simple as no breakfast and a pounding heart."

The doctor replaced Reid's chart. "You wanting company, or should I send the angry lady away?"

"Give me a minute."

"Will do. You get better now."

As soon as the doctor shut the door, the room was silent again, and Reid's chest felt a sudden tightness. But his monitors said he was fine. Only he knew he *wasn't* fine. Would he never ride again?

Unexpected tears pooled in his eyes, which he squinched tight until only a single tear dared to make a path down his face.

He thought he needed a minute, but every minute the world felt darker. With no answers until after the scans, with nothing to do, with a shooting pain every time he moved his head, he needed something, anything, to think about, besides what was spiraling in his head.

"Reid, hon?" Kellie's soothing voice felt nice inside.

He lifted a hand.

"Can we come in?"

We?

He lifted his hand again.

And then soft hands held it. Eden's hands. And moisture wet his hand. He squinted up at her.

Tears fell from her face. They fell from his face too.

Kellie stood beside her. "We've been really worried."

We, meaning Eden, no doubt. Though Kellie looked worried enough. She'd been through this whole mess with Ryan. But that didn't make it any less real the second time around.

"Hey." Eden met his eyes.

Kellie looked from one to the other.

"I promised not to yell at you." Her face held pain, and some embarrassment.

"Were you yelling?"

"That's not all she did." Kellie's eyes twinkled in amusement.

"Oh yeah?"

"She was out on the dirt."

He laughed in surprise, but it hurt.

"She was out there, running for you before they got the horse under control."

"Did she bring her shotgun?"

Eden snorted. And he enjoyed the laugh he'd pulled from her.

"I didn't used to be so volatile. Ask anyone I work with. I'm a calm, organized individual."

"Except when you're triggered."

"Riiight. Which seems to be all the time when I'm with you."

He considered her. "Well, now. That ain't so bad, right?"

"I don't know. I can't tell."

Kellie laughed. "I think it's safe for me to leave for a second. You two all right in here?" She was asking mostly

Reid, so he said, "I don't think she's gonna hit me, but you never know."

Kellie's laugh as she walked out of the room warmed him.

"Are the guys here?"

"Yeah. They told me to come in first so they could fix whatever I broke." She covered his hand with her other. "You've got some great friends out there."

"They are."

"I'm sorry I was yelling at you."

"Which time?"

Her smile grew again. "All the times, I guess."

"They don't know if I'll ride again."

"I know." Her breath shuddered and he could tell his pain was really getting to her too. And that was nice. Real nice. "Hey now. If I'm not crying, you don't need to be."

"You sure you're not crying?" She wiped at that pesky tear track that must have lingered down by his jawline.

"I don't know what you're talking about."

"They're bringing in the best doctor. If you've got anything going on that shouldn't be, Dr. Franco will know."

"Hey, thanks for that."

"You're welcome. And if we can pick up our fundraising, maybe we'll even discover something more useful in our lifetimes."

She'd included herself in that hope, and he remembered that she had a concussion too. He squeezed her hand in his. "Thanks for being here."

"You're welcome."

"When do you go back?" His memory was fuzzy. He knew it was soon.

"Couple days. I can delay maybe two more, but everything is starting to pick up again. I think this bill is gonna pass. We've had incredible momentum just in the last few days. Congress is almost back in session…" She paused. "Sorry. All of that probably sounds like an oatmeal bowl of information that has no use at all to you."

"No, it's great. It's important to you. I support you. I'm on the board of your non-profit, remember?"

"Oh, that's right." She opened her mouth, but then shut it again.

"Maybe we should let the guys in." He yawned. And his eyes closed. "Can't open them very well. Sorry." All of a sudden what he wanted most in the world was to sleep.

"Okay. I'll just go get them."

Her lips on his forehead surprised him. He fluttered open his eyes and smiled. "Now that's what a man really needs. Any time you want to put those lips on me, you're more than welcome."

"Oh you." She let go of his hands, and this time the quiet in the room felt nice.

Chapter 22

Eden avoided the hospital room for the next two days. She told herself, and others, that she was busy with work, that she was packing up to go back home, that she was finishing up her therapy assignments, that she was tired, that he wouldn't want to be disturbed, that … so many excuses had left her lips, she no longer knew which ones held an ounce of truth.

But she was flying home in the afternoon, and Reid was still at the hospital. So she needed to make her way over there right away. She lugged her suitcase to the front porch and piled all her belongings right there on top of it. Then she checked her watch. Just enough time to stop in to see him and then off to the airport to get there a little early.

She wiped her hands down the front of her jeans. They hadn't even defined their relationship, and she didn't think she could while he was in the hospital. Should she just leave? Without knowing where they stood? She clutched the key to his truck in her palm. Did it mean something to him that he'd told her to use it?

Probably. Kellie had thought it significant enough that she teased her about it now and then. "A man's truck is like lending his home. You just moved in, girl." Her laugh made Eden smile, but kind of broke her heart a little bit too. She wasn't moving in. She was moving away, and didn't know when she'd ever see him or this lovely town or her new friends again. Would she come out to visit her parents? Probably, but not for any length of time.

She'd hugged each of the women last night during their movie night. Some had already left. She'd clung to Kellie for an embarrassingly long hug, until the woman had to step back and remind her she could call. Eden had nodded. "Right. Thank you."

Now all that was left was Reid.

But her feet would not move toward his truck.

Another truck pulled into the driveway a bit fast, she thought, then slid to a stop, sending gravel dust up into the air. Kellie would not be pleased if they'd just powdered her flowers.

The other five of the Original Six hopped out of the truck.

"She's still here!" Eric called, and jogged over to her.

Before she could take two breaths, she was surrounded by one heck of a wall of cowboys. "Hey, guys."

"We wanted to catch you before you left." Ford nodded.

"Thanks. I'm heading over to the hospital now, actually, then to the airport. So this is a good time."

They shared looks with each other and Eden wasn't sure what they were after. "Well, it was great to get to know you guys." She stepped forward. "I guess this is goodbye."

But Eric surprised her, "No, stop that. We are not here for that nonsense."

She started to laugh but their serious faces gave her

pause. "Why are you here? Is everything okay at the hospital?"

"See, she cares about him," Ford pointed to her face.

"Of course I care. What's wrong?" The alarm grew. "Has something happened?" She looked from face to face and couldn't get a good read on any of them.

Finally, Ford shook his head. "He's fine. Sort of."

"No. He's not fine." Eric frowned. "He's miserable."

"Did he get some bad news?" She had been dreading the day a doctor told him he couldn't ride. So far, they had said only inconclusive things. And she had been beginning to suspect he might be cleared after all.

"He's just moping around, that's all." Westin shrugged, "His woman is leaving town. He's stuck in his bed. The man might have just lost everything he cares about."

"Except his land."

"True."

"And us. He didn't lose us."

"True again. But you're missing the point."

"Right. So, Eden. If you leave, and his rodeo goes, I just don't know what else he's gonna care too much about."

Her heart kind of melted and broke at the same time. She studied their faces. And she knew they meant well. But, what were they asking? For her to just...stay? Give up everything when she'd heard no promises from him, no inclination that they would even have a relationship, and if they did, what kind of relationship would it be if it required her to give up all that she'd worked for in the fight for the vets? "I think he knows where to find me." She smiled, hoping to keep the conversation light. "And he has my phone number."

They seemed to relax a bit more. "So you're not about to go break up with the guy?"

She'd been considering it, yes, but she shook her head, deciding right then to leave things vague. "Not at all. I don't think anything definitive needs to be said." They were going to be living over a thousand miles apart with completely different lives, but what she'd said was true. He was welcome to call and visit or whatever. It was possible, she supposed. Everything about this conversation was starting to weigh on her in heavy ways.

Lars unlooped his thumbs from his belt loops. "Well, then we just came to say goodbye I guess." He pulled her into a hug, smelling of soap and clean clothes. *Mm.* She could get used to this whole cowboy thing in her life. Most of all Reid. She tried not to show it, but the thought of leaving and not knowing when she'd see Reid again was really tearing at her insides.

One by one she hugged these larger-than-life gentlemen she'd come to know. "Thanks guys. I'm so happy to know each one of you."

"Oh, and we're here to drive you to the airport."

"Thanks. So should I just come back here with the truck?"

"Yep. And we'll get you there on time."

She nodded.

They all took seats on the front porch and watched while Eden made her way to his truck. As she was climbing in, she thought she heard one of them say, "She sure makes that truck look good."

"Way prettier than Reid."

With a grin, she closed the door, waved, and then backed up before pulling out of the long driveway.

Nerves were doing a number on her by the time she walked into the hospital and made her way to his room.

As she approached his door, a doctor's voice from

inside, Dr. Larsen's, said, "I agree with Dr. Franco. The man is an expert for a reason. If he thinks you're cleared, then I say give it a try. I would recommend easing back in. Maybe a week break and then some gentle practices."

"And we still don't know what happened?"

"No. Your scan shows a mild concussion. So it could be that. We're only right now learning more about the far-reaching effects of this kind of brain damage."

"I mean, doc. I fell and hit a rock."

"Sometimes that's all it takes."

Her guilt resurfaced. He hit a rock because Bear had knocked him down.

What had possessed her dog to do that? He typically did not jump up on people. He could even probably be fine with her when she went back to DC, but she couldn't bring herself to take him from all this land. At least her parents would be taking care of her dog for the time being. She was going to miss him, but he really wouldn't be happy in Arlington by himself in her apartment all day.

She stepped up to the door. "Knock knock."

The doctor looked nervous when he saw who had come, but she laughed. "No worries. No repeats of the first time we met."

"Hmm." He closed the charts. "So, one more day here just to get that final test result and then you're free to go."

"Thank you, doctor."

He nodded and slipped past her and out the door.

"Hey, stranger." She smiled as she stepped in.

He was sitting up, fully dressed, his blue flannel just making him all the more appealing in her mind. Cozy. What would they think if she climbed up into that bed beside him?

"Hey, you." His expression looked pained. "You heard?"

"Yeah, that's good news, right?"

"I think so? Last time you were skeptical and turns out you were right."

"You're wondering if I'm still as worried about it?" She shrugged. "Not if both doctors are saying the same thing. I mean, there's obviously a reason you passed out. But I think he's right. Ease back in. Pay attention to yourself. And maybe it will all come to nothing. There might be a championship in you yet." She sat beside him and took his hand.

"You're leaving."

Her nod felt grim. Her voice was stuck in her throat. But she met his gaze.

"For how long?"

Surprised, she hadn't considered this question. "Well."

"Maybe you could come out for the groundbreaking on the house." His words had come out hurried.

"Um, sure. Send me the dates and things."

"And for another rodeo or something?"

"Reid."

He exhaled slowly. "Don't even say it."

"Say what?"

"That this is over."

"I'm not. I'm just. Well, think about it. How excited are you to come out and live in DC?"

He snorted. "Not at all."

She waited for his words to sink in.

"But you're so happy here. You love the rodeo and the land and the ranch…"

"I have been on a therapy trip. I have a life, a career, a cause, you know how much all that means to me. You're on the board for goodness sake." She had been hoping something of his responsibilities would sink in. The chair had emailed that he could really use some help.

"I know." He adjusted his position on the bed so he was turned more toward her. "But I hate that place. You hate it too. You even said so. I can't live out there."

"And I can't give it up. We are on the brink of a bill that has taken me five years to put together. Five. Years." Her throat started to feel thick.

"So you're just gonna walk away from here like none of this happened?"

"No, look, why am I the bad person here? I'm merely going back to work, it's what people do. How come no one is asking you to quit rodeo?"

"You could though. You could do your job from anywhere. I can't do rodeo anywhere."

"No, but you do it everywhere. It doesn't matter if I'm here. Pretty soon you'll be in Utah and Wyoming and Dallas. You and I both know there's no good solution here."

"So you are breaking up." He leaned his head back.

"I'm not."

"Just 'cause you don't want to say the words, but you're not coming back."

The words caught in her mouth. "I'm not sure when I can. I've got six months of work waiting for me."

He nodded. "So it's goodbye."

"My flight leaves in a couple hours."

She scooted over so she could sit right beside him, and he pulled her as close as he could. They sat in silence for a time and then he kissed her forehead. "Let me stand up and say goodbye properly."

"You sure? You can stay in bed."

"I'm fine. They don't even know what's wrong with me."

As soon as they were both on their feet, he pulled her into his arms. His lips were insistent, his kiss full of hurting, his mouth sad. And she felt the ache go through her. Her hands clung to him, her body wished for more. But she knew the longing would only get worse, so she pulled away, "Goodbye, Reid. Call me, okay?"

"Sure."

She looked back only one more time before she walked out of his hospital room.

Chapter 23

Reid tried to focus on getting well enough to ride, because anytime he thought about anything else, his mind crowded with thoughts of Eden. And that was about as unproductive as trying to bareback a docile horse.

Which was what he'd also been doing. Jose thought it a good idea to ease him in on the old gentle horses. And if they kicked in the air one time, Jose was considering it a great victory. But he kept his mouth shut. Last time he'd rushed things and blown his big chance in front of the whole town.

But the town people were sympathetic. He was still getting home baked goods and treats at the arena left for him from all the people in Lost Creek. They were good people.

He told himself he and Eden were gonna call every night or at least check in now and again, but it was just too hard to talk to her on the phone when he'd been used to living under the same roof. And she was incredibly busy now. He could hear it in her voice. She was distracted when he caught her home, and he was too. And their lives were so different. He wasn't sure what to even ask her about.

And nothing was great. The other guys were doing great in their events. They were winning all over and qualifying for larger and better rodeos. Even Ryan was moving along as chute boss. Someone even called him boss the other day on their chat.

And Reid had nothing.

At least that's what it felt like.

He stepped out of the trailer to see José heading his way. By the look of the man's face, the news wouldn't be good.

"Reid. We're moving out. Tomorrow."

"Great. I'm already packed and ready to go. Where we headed?" This was news to him. But not unwelcome. He could use new air, distraction.

"You're not coming."

A hole seemed to open up in his gut. "What?"

You're staying here, working with some guys until you get better and safe and you can meet up wherever we are, however long it takes."

"No, José. This is gonna kill me."

"I've already decided. This is a short-term thing. They needed a team, and we got the guys here already gathered. I'm pulling up a new guy to ride bare."

Reid's face dropped. "You can't do that."

"I can. Look. That's how it is. You're young. But this is what happens. Guys get hurt. New guys ride, until they get hurt. It was bound to happen."

"But I'm not washed up. I'm coming back. Doc said so."

"Great. Take it slow and show me. Until then, I got a guy. And you're staying put. Lucky we're in Lost Creek. They said you can stay here as long as you need."

He nodded, but the news was not comforting and didn't sound lucky to him. "So if I ride and I ride good, I can come as early as next week?"

"Sure, but I don't want you rushing this. One more stunt like the last one and I'm not putting you back up on a horse ever. I got fans to answer to, sponsors, the whole deal. You keep getting hurt, you start to make us all look bad."

Wow. He'd never felt more like a number, like an asset, than he did in that moment. Only he wasn't really even an asset. They just didn't care. The Original Six. Down to four. No. He was not out. "I'm coming. I'll be out in three weeks."

"Great. Show me. Show me ten successful rides without falling off the horse and I'll take you back. You had a bright year ahead of you. I was thinking world. Believe me, I want you back as much as you want to get there. But I gotta be practical."

"Yeah, I guess so."

José turned around and started barking orders, maybe not even realizing he'd left Reid totally gutted. He fell into the nearest chair, still set up around the firepit outside his trailer.

He watched the entire rodeo pack up around him and leave. Then he climbed up onto Sundance and wandered about at a walk. The cleaning crew had also come through. And now the only things left to remind anyone of the rodeo that had been there were his trailer, his horse, some training horses Coach had let him borrow, and his sorry self.

The guys had come to say goodbye and they were full

of hope. The last thing Ford shouted as they drove away, all in the same truck, was, "See you in three."

Would they?

Chapter 24

Eden watched as their bill, House 4562 Aid for Vets, was read onto the floor. Every moment documented in her mind, every word a thrill. She'd worked tirelessly with the representative's aid to help draft the thing. She'd found all the expert sources. She had even drummed up the votes. She and her team. Tonight would be a night to celebrate with Vets 4 Life.

And then weeks more work to make sure nothing stood in its way. This bill was going to change lives. And she was going to watch it happen.

Nigel, the chair of their board, stood beside her. "We could use some more volunteers. Especially for the phones. Whatever happened to that guy for our board? Mr. Browning promised us someone."

Reid.

"I heard he got injured. We might still see him." Though she doubted very much he'd ever show his face in DC unless forced, and she wasn't going to be the one to do that.

"Well, maybe we can get more like him, you know, the faces to make the board look good and some real work horses."

"You worried about votes?"

"No, funds."

She nodded. "Always."

They stayed to see and be seen and thank all those who were involved. Then he left to prepare for the celebration for Vets 4 Life that night.

The day went from good to better as the congratulations poured in and the next steps were mapped out. As happy as she was about the way things were working out, she missed Reid. Plain and simple.

But there was nothing she could do about it now. People did long distance relationships all the time. Maybe she'd just have to start calling him more, or something. So far, she hadn't had a weekend off. And from the sound of things, last time she talked to Reid, he was desperately trying to get himself back on a horse.

She couldn't believe the team had just left him behind in Lost Creek. That felt a little heartless and much different from the vibe she'd gotten while she lived there. Those three weeks had seemed like moments in a quaint small town fairytale. Sometimes she had to ask herself if it all really happened.

A text came in. "*Drinks to celebrate*?" From a guy she mostly did not respect, but he'd worked hard and had turned into a valuable ally.

She was about to text a thumbs up but then he sent, "And breakfast if good turns to oh so good?"

She gagged. Like a real instant reflex. And then texted, "*Dang I've got plans. Thanks for all your help though.*" Hopefully that would be good enough.

And then a text from Reid. "*I heard the good news. Well done! You deserve all this and more. Want to celebrate?*"

"*Yeah.*" Maybe FaceTime with Reid was all she was gonna get.

"*You sure you don't have plans with that guy in the red tie?*"

Another one of the aids approached. He had been a huge help. He was wearing a red tie. She spun around, looking everywhere for Reid. He was here?

But she high fived this guy. Something about him seemed so young. But she was grateful for his help. "Hey, Grant. We did it, right?"

"*You* did it, Eden. I've never seen someone work so hard for something."

Her phone was going nuts. A million dings and vibrations.

"I couldn't have done it without the help. You know how it works."

"Yeah, I'm looking forward to pushing this thing through. Hey, you got plans tonight?"

Her phone kept dinging.

"Sounds like maybe yes? Can I take you to lunch sometime this week?" He tried again.

"Sure, we have so much to go over. Let's just get started, right?"

"Oh, well, yeah. But I was thinking maybe set that aside and this lunch could be non-working?"

She still tried to find Reid, but he was as elusive as ever. She didn't dare look at her phone with Grant right in front of her.

"Oh? Oh. Um. Sure. Why don't you call me and we'll set it up." At this point she just wanted to ditch Grant and find Reid. She laughed when her phone rang.

"Sounds like you have something going down." Grant's smile was genuine at least, not offended. "I'll call you later."

"Yeah, sorry about that."

"No. This is your moment, drink it all in. You deserve it."

As soon as he turned his back, her phone was at her ear. "Are you here?"

"Of course I'm here. I just read our new bill onto the floor of the house." A voice that was definitely *not* Reid's answered.

"Representative Hopkins. I'm so sorry. I didn't know it was you."

"I'm just kidding. I'm standing here with Mr. Browning's son, who I just learned is a friend of yours. I think you'd much rather be talking to him."

"Oh well, no, sir. Thank you again for sponsoring such an important bill."

"My pleasure. We'll get this thing passed and make history together. In the meantime, this young guy in a suit looks like he wants his phone back."

She laughed. Representative Hopkins was on Reid's phone. She didn't even know what to do with this collision of worlds.

"Uh, hello?"

"It's me now." *Reid.* He sounded so much happier, and present. She could hear the same sounds in the background of his phone as hers.

"Where are you? I can't spin around one more time looking for you."

"You can't see me? I'm taller than everyone here and twice as manly."

"Did you wear your hat?"

"No, my head's lonely for it too." He stepped out from around a corner. "I thought I'd dress the part."

Her mouth went dry. Like the Texas dirt. He looked amazing in a navy blue suit. Of course he did. The blue stretched across broad shoulders. His hair was trimmed, sharp and short around his ears. He carried a drink from one of the passing trays and if she didn't know better, he looked every bit like he belonged in this town. He stepped closer and then pulled some flowers from behind his back. "I got you something."

"What!" She pulled them close and smelled the roses. "These are gorgeous." She stepped closer. Did they hug? Kiss like she wanted to? In front of all these people?

"Don't look at me like that, woman. I can't be held accountable for what might happen next."

"Oh? And what's that?" She stepped closer.

"I'll be showing every man here who keeps looking your way just what I think about them trying to step in where they don't belong."

She laughed. Loud enough more people glanced their way.

"Who else do we need to thank?" He stood taller and adjusted the fit of his jacket.

"You saying you're willing to work the room with me?"

"I am. Especially if it will get us out of here sooner."

"Now that sounds more like the Reid I know."

"Admit it. You want to get out of here too."

"Oh yes I do. And you'll be happy to know I already went the rounds. We can leave right now."

"Say no more." He placed his hand at the small of her back and they both half walked, half ran from the room.

Once out on the street, the Capitol building looming up above them on the hill, Reid tapped a few times on his phone and a black sedan pulled up to the curb. He held open the door.

"What's this?"

"This. Is our ride."

"Nice." She slid in and he was right beside her, as close as possible. He laced their fingers together and then kissed her forehead. "More later." His ridiculous eyebrow wiggle made her laugh again. Everything in her world seemed more perfect than it had ever been all of a sudden. Because Reid showed up?

She couldn't believe her own reactions. But why not? He was the best man of any she knew.

He was watching her. "Where to, big shot?"

"What? Wherever."

"Don't you have someplace you have to be right now? Congratulatory party?"

"Vets 4 Life is throwing a party for all the volunteers, but they have that covered. I thought about getting drinks for a second."

"But the guy turned out to be a jerk."

"What? No. I just hadn't totally decided yet."

"Hm. And so right now, on the day you pass the biggest and most important bill of our administration, you are completely free?"

"I guess so." She smiled and then turned to him. "I'm just so happy you're here. I would have made myself free."

"Words I'd give anything to hear again and again and again." He lifted his chin and leaned forward to the driver. "Can you take us to Spices?"

"You got it."

"How about dinner?"

"Dinner would be great. And, Reid. Are you gonna tell me what's going on? How are you here?"

"I wouldn't miss this. It's the most important day of your year. I watched it read and everything."

"You didn't tell me."

"I wanted to watch your face." He grimaced. "Does that sound cheesy? Or creepy?"

"A bit stalkerish," she laughed. "But no. I'm so glad you were there."

"Yep. And when I saw that joy; it lit your whole face. I was just so dang proud of you."

She felt her cheeks heat. "Wow." She hadn't expected to see or hear from him today. And him in DC, wearing a blue suit, being super charming, was doing things to her, even more powerful things than his whole cowboy self had done.

She turned away.

"What's this?" He leaned forward, trying to get her attention back.

"I'm just…It's so good to see you. But I know you're gonna leave." Her throat felt full as she said it, which was so ridiculous. But it did. She couldn't help it if she'd had a really full and emotional day.

He pulled her even closer. "I know. Don't think about it yet. I have a whole night."

One night. She nodded. "Well then, this is gonna be the best night of our year."

"Definitely."

Dinner was amazing. Somehow Reid had picked the most delicious Thai Asian fusion place in Bethesda. She stopped at licking her plate, but it was that good.

They laughed the entire dinner. It was as if Reid was determined to make her smile, and it worked.

"So then Bear comes to see me."

"What!" She couldn't believe what she was hearing.

"Yep. Somehow on one of their visits, your parents got

wind of my lonely self, hanging out at the arena all by myself. But I have to admit, when that animal came running, I ducked."

"I don't blame you one bit." She was…she didn't even know what she was. "So you and my parents?"

"Yeah. They brought me dinner and we sat at my fire for a bit." He laughed. "They're good people. I see you all over them."

"Wow. I'm so happy they did that." She hadn't even thought to tell her folks Reid was there alone. They didn't know much at all about Reid, only that Mr. Browning's son was in Lost Creek. She felt a little bit like she'd dropped the ball, but someone was picking it up. Kellie maybe?

"So, your mammoth beast is fine. He sat at my feet the whole time and only whined for you once."

She moved closer to him in the crook of his arm at their bench. "I miss Bear."

"If I tell you I whine for you too, will I get an I miss you?"

She looked up into his face, drinking in every feature and then sighed. "I miss you every day. I wish there was a solution."

He didn't answer, just pressed his lips to the top of her head.

And she said nothing more, because what could be said?

Chapter 25

Reid and Eden walked along together, hand in hand along the Tidal Basin near the Mall in Washington, DC. They'd just left the Jefferson Memorial and then the FDR. Eden had taken ridiculous pictures of him and the dog statue in front of FDR. Even though his feet were starting to ache, the night was beautiful and he was not ready to let her go.

Their hands swung together side by side.

She turned to him, feet skipping a little. She was obviously not as tired. "Have you seen the World War Two Memorial yet?"

He wanted to say no, so he could pretend to let her show it all to him as if for the first time. But he couldn't lie to those large hopeful eyes. "I've seen it." He sighed.

"Oh true. You actually live here, don't you?"

"Sort of. I mean, I now own land outside of San Antonio and my trailer is still parked in Lost Creek, but I was raised here. Maybe I should call it home."

"I would not complain if you did." She didn't look at

him, but he knew what she was saying. And he didn't respond. That was a lot to respond to. He still had a rodeo to compete in before he could do anything like claim DC as home again.

He'd ridden a full ride, on a tough horse without a single problem, and his time had been half decent too. When he called the boss, José had told him to high tail it back to the team immediately. He had taken a quick detour to see Eden first.

But the night had gone too quickly, and it really was about time to get the car and take Eden home. As soon as they made it back to the road, he texted their driver. "I don't even want to say this but…"

"But it's time to go home?" She squeezed his hand. "That's the worst."

"It is the worst." He laughed. "But hearing you say that, knowing you miss me too, makes leaving so much easier." They moved to a bench and he sat his tired legs down. "I'm remembering now how in shape you are."

"Oh my gosh. I forgot about that. How long were you following me that day?"

"Pretty much the whole way around the basin. And you were booking. I've never run at that pace."

"Wow, I was stressed that day. I kept up the death pace to help fight all my worries about this bill, and Vets 4 Life and more volunteers…Now it seems like pointless worry since it all came together so well."

"But there's more work to do, right?"

"Yes. Always."

"I'll come back and help."

Her eyes lit. "Can you?"

"Well, I'm finally okay to ride again. But we don't compete every weekend. I can practice through the week and fly here now and then to do the job my dad promised I would."

"That would be amazing." She leaned closer and kissed his cheek.

And that was all he needed for encouragement to pull her close into his arms, cradling her before pressing his lips to hers. "I tried to keep up because I thought you were hot."

She laughed against his mouth. "What?"

"I thought you were hot." His grin softened the fire of his words and made her grin.

"Is that why you were following me?"

"Partly." He laughed. "At the time I wouldn't have admitted it at all, but I was really impressed with you. I wanted to know what makes you tick, why you do the things you do, and…It really got under my skin how much you hated me."

She kissed him again, maybe trying to stop his questions, but he refused to be sidetracked. "Why did you hate me so much?"

She shook her head. "Now, come on. Hate is a strong word. I have never, ever, hated you."

"Okay, but you know what I mean, then. Whatever amount of loathing you felt for me, where did it come from?"

He watched her struggle to answer, and he wondered what could be so difficult.

"I just thought you were such a womanizer. A careless kind of man, just like every other guy I see here in DC all the time."

He nodded slowly at first, but then his grin grew. "And that's why it's so awesome you came out to Lost Creek.

"Oh? And why is that?"

"Because then and there I proved just how different I am from anyone out here." He laughed. "Probably not in the ways you were hoping, but all the same."

"And just how are you different?"

He waved his arm out across everyone around them. "How many cowboy hats do you see walking around?"

"Not a one."

"And how many boots?"

"None."

"And that, my dear Eden Cooper, is a crying shame."

"You know, I think you're right."

"So, I may have come across strong..." He side eyed her and then laughed when she snorted.

"At first." She shrugged. "And I may have come across too angry."

"But look at us now." He put his arm across her back. "You cold?"

"No, I'm just right, actually. More than right. Time with you makes everything better." She looked up into his face. "Maybe that sounds silly."

"Nope. That's exactly how I feel. This time right here is gonna keep me going for another few months."

"Is that how long it's gonna be?" She seemed to deflate right in front of him.

"I don't know." Their car arrived, so he stood. "That's the worst part about all this. I don't know."

He closed the door after she got in and moved around to the other side of the car. He could come. He just had to look at his schedule to determine which weekends he could come help out with Vets 4 Life. It was a priority now that he'd seen her again. Missing Eden was like losing the rodeo itself. Even though he'd come to grips with the fact that one day he'd have to retire from rodeo, he couldn't live without Eden.

He sat in the car beside her. Eden gave her address to their driver and then moved over so that she was pressed against him. She rested her head on his shoulder and pulled his hand into her lap. While toying with his fingers, she said, "I'm not ready for tonight to be over."

"I don't think I'll ever be ready for that."

"Have you been writing in your journal?"

He nodded. He'd been writing about her mostly. But the times he'd worked through some of the stuff about his dad were helpful. He was having breakfast with him tomorrow morning.

"I'd like to share some of mine again, if you have time. You could come up for a bit."

"Sure." Any excuse to linger a moment was a good one in his mind. And he realized how important this journaling was to her and her recovery. "Did you learn anything new?"

"Maybe a little bit. And this time it was something good, important."

They pulled up to her apartment building and climbed out. "I live on the fifteenth floor."

He tipped his head back and whistled through his teeth. "How many floors are there?"

"Thirty." She laughed. "And now you sound like you're from Lost Creek again."

"Well, I am. As well as here. But I've never lived in Arlington. And I don't go to New York very often, so these huge apartment buildings are new to me."

"That makes sense. For a guy who lives outside Langley." She rolled her eyes.

"Now, hold on. Nothing wrong with where I live."

"Not at all. You just can't be expected to have a realistic understanding of how the rest of the world lives."

"Says the woman who lives in a half a million-dollar apartment." He raised his eyebrows in challenge.

"I'm renting. And it's not even close to half a million."

"Hm."

They got in the elevator, and he pulled her close. "The verbal sparring with you is incredibly appealing. But tonight, I just want the connection. I miss you when you aren't right here."

She brought her hands up to his neck. "Then I should probably just stay here."

"If only you could." The lips he pressed to hers were tender. He couldn't hide his longing, but he didn't lengthen the kiss either.

They exited out onto her hallway. The air smelled of curry. A long, carpeted hall led to a floor length window on the opposite end. She stopped partway down and turned a key in her lock.

The door opened to a wall of windows. It was classically furnished. Large, overstuffed chairs and a sofa. A bookshelf. An end table. And the windows. He whistled. "This is incredible."

He stepped close to the edge, his bones tingling from the height. "And I thought the water tower was high."

She called from the other room. "Make yourself comfortable. There are drinks, waters, in the fridge."

He could see Highway One, the Iwo Jima Memorial and even the Washington Monument from her window.

"Is that the Pentagon? I think I see the Pentagon."

She came back out with two water bottles and her journal. "Come here, you."

"How do you not just stand here staring every day?"

"I think I do." She laughed. "It's beautiful with everything lit like it is right now, but it's also beautiful in the daytime, especially now, in the spring and in the fall. Wait till you see the leaves change."

"You think I might get to see the leaves from up here in the fall?" He turned to join her on the couch.

"Well, I hope you will."

He took the water she offered because he suddenly needed it, like he needed more of that kiss he'd tasted in the elevator.

She snuggled next to him.

But he shook his head. "This is not how we share from our journals."

"What?"

He turned his body so he was leaning against the arm rest and then pulled her back against his chest. "Remember? This is how we share from our journals."

She rested her head against him. "I wish it could always be just like this."

His chin fit nicely on top of her head.

"Tell me what you learned about your dad."

He hadn't expected his dad to be a part of the conversation, not really. But he thought about him for a minute. "I think I get him better now. I've always known that he just wanted what's best for me. I get that. I have just always kind of thought he obviously doesn't know what I need, because I am so happy out in Texas, and so unhappy thinking about trying to live his life that I just always assumed the man doesn't get me. And his lack of respect for what I want to do with my life has hurt me."

She nodded against him.

"And I think that's what I realized. It hurt my feelings.

And then I got to thinking about *his* feelings. I think me refusing his lifestyle and all the connections and help he offered hurt him too. It's not a small thing he offered me. And I have a law degree because of him. And I could work anywhere in the world or on the Hill if I wanted to. How many people could say that?"

"Sometimes I forget all about your law background."

"It's not something I like to get around," he admitted. "I listen to you talk about all the good you want to do, the change you hope to make. You have a bill on the House floor right now. And I'm impressed by all that. I see my dad in a new way. And then I get up on Spitfire and knock myself around for eight seconds before I fall off." He shook his head. "And I love it. I realized I can't make myself love what he does, but I respect it. And even though I'm not making widespread change in our country, good comes of my riding."

"It's difficult to break outside of the government bubble and still feel like things matter."

"Exactly."

"If I leave, will I be missing out on the city where everything happens? Will I lose my edge? My influence?" She shook her head. "But there are plenty of people doing good things everywhere."

His arms circled closer around her. "What did you discover in your journal?"

"I think I finally wrote down every hard memory from Iraq. And there were a lot. Stuff I had forgotten. Horrible smells, thoughts, sounds of people calling out for help. Lots of explosions. No wonder I have brain injuries. So many things I don't want to remember." She lifted her journal. "They're all in here now." She ran a hand over the leather.

"But Kellie had asked me to write a 'So what' page. And I could write more than one. But to begin a section where I think about what these experiences mean to me. What they will do to help me in my life. Because obviously they changed me. But so what? What will I do with that change?"

Reid loved that. "Maybe I should go to Kellie. That's a great idea for mine too."

"It was this section I wanted to share." She flipped through pages, not seeming too anxious to linger in some of it, then stopped on a spot toward the end. "Do you mind if I read it to you?"

He nodded against her head. "I want to hear everything you want to tell me."

She took a minute to start. He wondered if she was having second thoughts about sharing something so personal. But he just waited. This stuff was tough to work through, and probably even more tough to speak out loud.

"Why did I serve in the first place?" Her voice was soft, but clear. He held perfectly still.

"I knew it would be traumatic. Of course, I could never know how much or what specifically I would have to deal with." She ran her finger along the page for a moment. He couldn't see the words as they were hidden from him behind her shoulder.

"And if I hadn't served, I would never know these awful memories. I would be like most other women I know, shielded from the sights that haunt my dreams. And sometimes that sounds nice. But I would never want to be those women. I would never want to be the person who obliviously lives their free lifestyle without once acknowledging where it comes from. I wouldn't want to be the woman who goes for a run, takes out her bike, or hikes a mountain but never knows what her body could really do. I never want to be the American who lives day to day, happy that someone else was willing to do that hard thing." She shook her head while she read, "I feel strong. Some of the proudest moments of my life are those I spent in Iraq. And maybe I couldn't save that little boy, or any of the others, but I was the last person to look them in the eye and love them." She shuddered and wiped at her tears. "Just let me finish this, sorry."

He held her closer, trying to give her strength.

"And I'm not God. I realized I had no control over any of this. But what I could do, I did. Even though it's hard to accept that I couldn't save some, that things weren't perfect, I accept that I did my part. And that is something to carry with me as a triumphant victory." The breath that left her told him she was finished.

He kissed the top of her head, breathing in the clean smell in her hair, something related to lemons maybe. And he just held her.

After a few minutes, she closed the journal. Then she rotated in his arms and turned to face him. "For the first time, I get it. I get how I've been feeling and that last bit, knowing I'd do it again, knowing I would never want to be like everyone else—that gets me." She touched her heart. "And besides that, I like to feel strong. Really strong."

He thought she was strong in many more ways than simply physically, but he knew now was not the time to share those thoughts. Maybe someday he could help her see her other strengths as well. But for now, he allowed what she'd just taught him to sink in. "I'm sorry I tried to take away some of that feeling of strength by trying to do things for you."

Her beautiful mouth turned up in a smile. "I understand you better now. Most of the time, I would love for you to do the strong things."

"But I just need to understand the difference."

She nodded, then rested a hand on his arm. "Thank you, for listening. Kellie said sharing will take the healing one more step, and she's right. But you're the only person I wanted to share any of this with."

He reached out and adjusted the hair that had fallen in her face, then ran his fingers down her beautiful neck and shoulder. "It's important to me that you would open up to me like that. I want to always be this safe place for you."

Then she shifted closer. "And now I'm having a hard time ignoring that you're here, in my apartment, and so…available."

His smile grew, but before he could laugh, she'd stretched up, leaning against his chest, and placed her lips on his.

He responded immediately, pulling her closer, shifting her body, cradling her, loving her. His mouth covered hers, accepting her lead on where they would go. Accepting her kisses, each one sending him into waves of desire to roll her onto her back and take control of the situation. But he held back and accepted her gift, her expression of her love. And he knew tonight couldn't go any further.

When her lips were swollen, how he decided he most liked them, and her hair a mess, which he liked even more, he kissed her once more on her nose and then created some distance. "And now, my temptress. I'm going to stand up and walk out that door."

She fell back against the couch. "I hate this."

"I know." He had ideas, hope for something, but he

didn't say any of it. He wanted to make sure it really would work.

But she stood. And walked him to the door.

The hallway felt cold, dim, and lonely as he walked back to the elevator.

Chapter 26

This time, the separation with Reid felt much more hopeful. Their time apart, more bearable. Nothing had changed in their circumstances. No promises had been made. They weren't even official in any way. But the four weeks since he'd left had been filled with phone calls and texts to each other. Somehow, he was more a part of her life. Her phone dinged.

Good luck today.

She smiled and sent him a heart emoji. Today was an important board meeting. They were to discuss the upcoming year, upping their fundraising, and keeping the votes that had been promised for the bill to pass through the House. She still didn't have a solid person over fundraising. No one wanted to take that on. So she'd been passing the task around piecemeal, and it worried her.

The parking lot to the building for their office space was empty. In a town that worked long hours every day, this was a rare moment of quiet. And concerning because their meeting started in thirty minutes.

But no matter. She used her security badge to open the door, adjusted the temperature in their conference room, and tidied up a bit. They'd had some late-night food runs over the last week. Then she hooked her computer up to the presentation equipment and started to go over her notes.

When people began arriving, she felt ready and confident they were in a good spot to get this thing passed. She didn't usually attend the board meetings, leaving that to the chair. But today she had some good news. Somehow, they'd just received a huge donation from a new supporter. She had no connections with this company, but she was happy they had somehow become aware of their cause.

As people started to arrive, she met them at the door. "Thank you for being here." Those words, spoken to every person, felt important. And when they were all seated, she nodded to the chairman. "If I might take a minute first."

"Of course."

"I'm so happy to be with you today. I just wanted to make sure you knew that the grass roots efforts of this campaign are the most important. The moments in this room are what determine our success. And without each one of you, this bill would never have been introduced onto the floor." She went through each committee and praised their successes. "As for fundraising, we are still looking for a person to fill this position."

"Actually, Eden, as of this morning, we have a new volunteer for fundraising."

"Oh, that's excellent." The relief that filled her was probably obvious to all. She laughed. "Who is it?"

"Reid Browning. You remember that guy Browning placed on our board? His son? He's shown his face again and volunteered for the spot."

A new voice, Reid's, interrupted from the doorway. "I don't know yet if we can rely on him, but any new person willing to work should be given a shot, don't you think?" He stood in the doorway, leaning against the frame, and winked.

She stopped herself from running to embrace him. Instead, she looked him over critically. "Fundraising is a big job."

"And I'm a big guy."

"I see that." She huffed inside. Did he have to be so good looking and so ridiculous at the same time? Shaking her head, she recognized the very first thoughts she'd ever had about him. "Well, then, since we have just arrived at your spot on the agenda, maybe you'd like to take some time?"

He dipped his head. "I thought you'd never ask."

She took her seat.

And then he amazed her by taking out a laptop from his briefcase. "Do you care if I plug this in?"

"Not at all." Honestly, she didn't think up until this moment that the man owned a laptop.

Once his documents were up, she did a quick scan and opened her mouth in amazement.

"As you can see, we have a good list of potential donors. Here in the first column are those who have already donated. But they haven't been approached again since the entrance of the bill to the floor. We will start by giving them a call to thank them and letting them know about a new tier of donation level. I think we can safely assume a significant increase from a number of these. In this column here are some potential donors." He went through the corporations and individuals one by one.

The list was huge and, in many cases presumptuous. "Where did you come up with these particular targets?"

"Many of them are close friends or competitors with those already donating." He raised one eyebrow, almost in challenge.

And she couldn't help but grin. So, he had something to prove.

"And the others are some connections I happen to have. And some from those in this group." He turned to the chairman. "For example, I noticed that your aunt sits on the board of this major conglomerate."

Nigel sat forward, his dark eyes lighting. "You know, she does. I didn't think of her at all when we went through this the first time."

Reid continued down his columns and then proceeded to take them through a doable plan of action. "And then if we can work through this in a timely manner, a modest prediction of funds accumulated sits at this total here."

The number was astounding. More than she thought she would ever need.

"What will we do with the extra? We are a non-profit…"

Reid held up his hand. "If I may?" He clicked to another chart. "One idea. I was in a small town outside San Antonio and saw a sign. Wounded Warriors. When I looked them up, I saw similar goals, a similar mission, and equal passion for exactly what this board is working for. I say we work on unifying our efforts, spreading the word through the grass roots local communities, and building the footprint of Vets 4 Life all over the country. How many vets are suffering in silence because they are beyond our scope and reach?"

Nigel nodded and everyone in the group started to clap.

Eden stood and joined them in their applause. And then Reid sat.

"Thank you, Reid. I think I can offer each one of us as ready to receive our marching orders. Just tell us what to do and who to contact."

"I'll add to your press kits and get you a solid pitch this week."

She stood at the front of the room speechless. Who was this Reid? And where had her cowboy gone? But after staring at him an almost uncomfortably long time, she shook her head slightly and turned to the rest of her team. Their smiles were encouraging. The hope at an all-time high. "Well, after that, I don't think there's anything we can't do. You ready to sweep the country?"

They laughed, and then she moved on to the next agenda item.

Once they'd gone through all the rest of the bullet items, and the room had cleared except for Nigel and Reid, she held her hand out to Nigel. "Thank you for all you do on this board."

Reid stepped closer. "Yes, I want to introduce myself personally. I hope we can work well together."

"I think I speak for us both when I tell you how grateful we are to have you on board." Nigel moved to stand beside Eden.

"I'll take your gratitude any day. But no need to speak for Eden here. She can tell me herself."

Her smile grew and she recognized his claim to her attention, to her intimacy? Would he say something about them being officially…something? She placed a hand on Nigel's arm. "Reid and I are close."

Nigel nodded, slowly, and then with a tight smile,

turned to leave. "Well, great. Thanks again. I look forward to working with you."

Before he could leave, Reid walked him out. "Could we do lunch tomorrow? I know this great burger place. And you can wear jeans."

"I don't usually do jeans."

"That's okay. Guys with suits show up too. But I'm gonna need your advice about a lot of this stuff. I can insert confidence when necessary, but when it comes down to it, I need some help with execution."

Nigel perked up at that statement. And lunch was set.

Then, at last, Reid turned to her, the room empty but for them. He closed the door.

"What a surprise!" She stepped to him.

"I wasn't sure I could pull off some of those donors so I didn't want to tell you until I knew I could."

"And you just showed up? Took your spot on the board?"

"Looks like it."

"And your rodeo?"

"I'll be leaving soon to compete in Mesquite."

"And that's a big one, right?"

"One of the biggest."

"So, this is gonna work?" So much more rested behind her simple question. So much neither of them had the answer to.

"I think so." He reached for her and pulled her into his arms. "That's kind of something I wanted to ask you."

"Oh? Which part?"

"Is this—" He pointed to them both. "—Us, gonna work? Will you, Eden Cooper be my girlfriend? My one and only? Do you want me around in your business here?"

Her heart thrilled at the thought. "Yes, yes, and yes!" Then she laughed. "We have to try."

"Yes, we do." Then he reached for his briefcase. "And now, I'm sorry I can't linger here with you and do our typical route around the Tidal Basin, but I have work to do. I set up meetings with one of the larger potentials myself. With my father."

"Oh, that's awesome." She nodded. "Well, then you go at it."

He leaned in and kissed her, then wrapped an arm around her back. "This is what a man needs as some motivation to bring home the bacon."

She almost couldn't kiss him properly while laughing at his ridiculous joke, but his persistence, his lips moving over her own soon blocked out all other thought, except the one focused on him. Was this really happening? She hoped so.

Chapter 27

Reid worked hard for the few days he was in DC. He spent his evenings with Eden and his days drumming up support so that when he left Sunday night, things were set up to continue even though he wasn't in town. On the way to the airport, his father had surprised him and wanted to go with him. They didn't talk about anything remarkable, but things were comfortable between them. As he pulled up to the curb, his dad surprised him again and said, "I'm real proud of you, son. You've made your way in the world on your terms. And now, you're working on one of the most important things ever to pass through Washington. You've got some of the best people the Hill has to offer on your side and the trust and respect of a woman without compare. I could never have given you any of this." His voice caught and Reid recognized the hurt there. Hurt he might have caused.

"No, Dad. It was you. If I'd gone straight to Lost Creek with no education behind me, I could never have done any of this. I needed your connections, your experience out here. Dad. Make no mistake. I am the man I am, rodeo and all, because of you. Do you know what I think sometimes when I'm in the chute and that animal is bucking around beneath me, right before I ride?"

He laughed. "What?"

"I ask myself, what would my dad do?"

He laughed again but couldn't hide the new bit of moisture in his eyes. "Do you now?"

"I do, and when I think about my dad, there ain't an animal alive that can win out in that arena."

And then his dad pulled him tight. "Thank you, son. It's good to have you back."

"It's good to be back."

TWO WEEKS LATER, seats were filling for the Mesquite, Texas rodeo. Camera crews were getting set up. All major sports channels had announced their coverage. Reid was looking forward to it. All the Six were there, with five competing in their events. It seemed like half the town of Lost Creek had shown up to support. They held up signs now and then. "Original Six." "Lost Creek Represent." "Go SHC." But his family seats out in the arena were still empty. Still no sign of his dad or Eden.

"Don't let it mess with you." His boss showed up at his side. "Either they come or they don't, but they don't belong anywhere near your head when you get out there to ride."

"I know. If I see them now, I won't be looking later, that's all."

"I'll have someone checking for you. We'll send word if the seats fill."

He nodded, then worked his shoulders, with one eye on

the stands. He'd noticed a kink now and then, something tightening up when he rotated them.

"Want someone to work those out?" Jose was still hovering.

"Yeah. I think that would help." But before Boss could run off to get it figured out, he held out a hand to stop him. "But not now. I've got to go get out of my own head for a bit." He looked out over the stands one more time and then turned his back. They'd come. He'd just plan that they would. But either way, he was gonna win the event. If he never rode another year of his life, if this was it, he was going to win. He might keep riding, but he had no guarantees. He knew that now. And now, this moment, was what he was living. Now was his moment. Now.

He kept repeating inspirational things all the way to his room. He changed into his gear and by the time he'd exited out and made his way to the sidelines behind his chute, he'd almost forgotten about Eden and his dad. Almost.

He stood up on the railings, looking out into the crowd. He was at just the wrong angle to see his family seats.

But one of the hands ran up. "Jose said to tell you they're here."

Reid's heart thumped. "What?"

"They're here. The girl and your old man."

"Thank you." His smile grew and the tightness in his shoulders loosened. He rotated his arms. "Oh yeah, that's much better." Then he whooped. And with a big, "Yee-haw!" he swung his hat in the air and then replaced it on his head.

The announcer laughed into his microphone. "Sounds like our cowboys are ready to go. How about our audience?"

The crowd cheered in response, and Reid remembered once again why he loved the rodeo.

Event after event went by. Reid would be going second to last, right before Westin on a bull. He went to go find his guys. They were under the stands waiting for him.

"So did she finally come?" Eric clapped him on the shoulder.

"Yep, and my dad beside her." He couldn't stop the proud grin even if he wanted to. It was something so amazing to have people he loved there to see him. He sucked in a breath. People. He. Loved. "I think I love her." He looked from face to face in amazement.

Only they weren't amazed. In fact, they didn't even seem to care.

"Dude, of course you love her." Ford looked to the others. "Doesn't he?"

"Don't be looking at me. I'm not the one to know if a man's in love or not."

The others put their hands up, shaking their heads.

But Lars gripped his shoulder. "She's a keeper."

"Yeah, don't mess this up."

Before they could all give their different warnings about him not being a knucklehead he just said, "Got it."

Then they stepped together in their circle of six. They started with Ryan. "For God."

"Family."

"Country."

"Respect."

"Love."

"And the cowboy way."

They looped hands around shoulders and stood facing each other in their circle.

Reid loved these guys. Brothers. "We need wins tonight."

"We can advance if we do."

"And I need you to impress my girlfriend."

"Yeah, whatever."

Someone's alarm dinged.

Lars tapped a button on his phone. "Looks like I'm up."

They parted ways and Reid headed back toward his chute. It was being used for something else at the moment, but he liked to be nearby. Instead of stopping there though, he kept moving along the circle, hoping for a better angle for a sight of Eden and his dad. He stood up on the rails a bit further down. And then, sure enough, he could see his dad's profile and next to him, Eden. And they were laughing. His dad was so amused at whatever it was they were talking about, that his face looked like it might crack. And then he put his arm around Eden, giving her a side arm Dad hug. And Reid didn't think his world could get any sweeter.

He turned and at last was able to fully clear his mind, ready to ride.

Chapter 28

Reid's dad reminded her so much of Reid. He was smart, hilarious, charming, and attentive. She didn't know if Reid would want to hear this, but she could totally see where he got most of his drive and leadership. His father exuded a kind of friendly power. She didn't know what else to call it. She turned to him. "I wanted to thank you for sending Reid to be on the Vets 4 Life board."

"I'm happy to hear he's pulling his weight."

"Oh, so much more than that. He's taken us to the next level. It's amazing what that man can accomplish."

He sighed. "I know. The potential is there. I used to think he wasted it here." He shook his head. "But who am I to say? He's excellent at this too."

"He really is. I think they're all famous in the rodeo world." She laughed. "I'm learning more about it, and I think these guys are gonna win big tonight. They're expected to."

The announcer interrupted to call out the next event.

They watched every one, laughing and cheering and joining in with the crowd. And then the lights went low and flashed through the audience. "And now. We have a special treat for you. Here, for the bareback event, back from a crazy head injury, world record holder, Reid Browning!"

The crowds went crazy. Music played and the lights continued for a moment more. Then everything went quiet.

The buzzer rang and Reid's horse left the chute, kicking and leaping and jumping. Silently Eden counted with the clock.

"Wow, that horse is hardly on the ground." His father's hands clutched the arm rest.

She could well understand the sentiment.

The horse spun in the air, with one last bucking kick, but Reid held on. She had no idea how, but he held.

And then the buzzer rang again.

Reid slipped from the horse, but the animal kept on kicking. Instead of standing, he rolled out of the way and then scrambled up over the metal fencing.

The crowd laughed and pointed. But Reid's father and Eden both held their breath.

The clowns finally distracted the horse and ran it out of the arena. Then Reid tipped his hat.

The scores went up. And Reid whooped before he threw his hat up into the air.

The announcer shouted into his microphone. "He's done it! Reid Browning has beat his own world record, qualifying for a shot down in Houston."

Reid waved his hand in the air, then picked up his feet and ran the whole perimeter of the arena until he got to her and his dad. Then he took off his hat again and bowed before continuing his run around the arena and then out of the place.

The Jumbotron showed a laughing image of her face and then his father. She waved before the camera moved on.

Bull riding was up next. But all she could think about was how happy Reid had looked. And how she didn't want to miss any more moments like that one.

After the rodeo, and a long and hilariously fun dinner with Reid and his father and both her parents, she sat with him on the porch of her parents' house. Bear lay on the wood decking between them. And everything felt like it was right as it should be.

She couldn't wait another minute to tell him what she'd decided just that day during the rodeo.

"Reid."

"Eden."

They'd both spoke at the same time.

She waited. "What is it?"

"Can we go for a walk?"

"Sure."

Their hands came together naturally. The night air was warm enough. The bugs were not out yet. And their feet on the gravel driveway was the only sound.

"I think the road curves around to a pond," she offered.

But he suddenly seemed to be at a loss for words. At last he shrugged. "What were you gonna say?"

"Oh! Well, I decided something today."

"Something good?"

"I think so." She squeezed his hand. "I loved what you did for Vets 4 Life. I loved it. And you coming out there when you can, being able to see you there, it means so much. And then seeing you today. That was incredible. What if I'd missed that?" She shook her head. "I don't want to miss important things in your life. And I love it out here. My parents. My dog."

"I'm getting the feeling Bear is always gonna come first."

"Oh hush. So what I'm trying to say is, I want to be a part of your life, here, there, wherever. I've already looked up grass roots efforts here and out by your land, and there are two organizations that are well on their way to making a huge difference. I'd like to work with them and start a whole new grassroots effort like you talked about. But I'm gonna need to be out here much more often in order to do it."

"I'm liking the sound of this. Because it brings us to exactly what I wanted to talk to you about." Then he dropped down to one knee.

"Reid Browning, what are you doing?" She clutched at his hand. "Are you—?"

"I'm trying to ask you something here."

"Okay." She held her breath, but then felt faint. And he stayed silent. "What are you gonna ask, Reid?" He looked like he'd never speak again.

"I'm sorry. I just can't believe I'm here in this moment with you. I love you, Eden."

Tears immediately welled. "I love you too. Everything is better with you."

"And I am so happy to hear you say you want to be a part of my life. Because I decided something today too. I don't want to do any of this, not unless you're in it."

She nodded. "I plan to be. I'll come as often as I can—"

"And I want us to be one in all things. Not just visit back and forth. I'm down here on my knee. I want to marry you, Eden. Will you marry me? Will you be my wife and you can bring Bear if you have to and we'll go back and forth together and do what we can apart, and it will just be better than what we're trying to do right now."

His eyes were earnest, sincere, hopeful. The love she saw there felt magical. How could it be she was loved like that? She kneeled down with him. "Yes, Reid. I will marry you." The kiss that held his was full of promises, made and accepted. Then he stood and pulled her up with him, not pausing one second of their kiss. His lips captured hers with a fierce love that carried her away. The bristle on his chin itched at her, then his teeth nibbled her bottom lip and pulled it into his mouth. Running his tongue along her lower lip, she clutched at him, bringing her fingers up, digging them into the back of his head. "Mm. Reid."

"Hm?"

"Where's your truck?"

"Hm?" He paused, his eyes smiling at her. "You wanna make out in the back of my truck?"

"Would you rather my parents' house?"

And then he laughed. And she bristled.

And he immediately tried to get back some of what they had, but she shook her head. "Nope. Moment's gone." She started to walk back to the porch.

"Oh, wait, come on. Now where are you going?"

"I thought we'd give the news to my parents."

"We can take the truck out. The lookout is good for more than just looking." He wiggled his eyebrows, but she shook her head. "Reid."

"I just figure if you don't kill me first, we'll have a really happy time of it. Thank you for saying yes."

His words, so sincere, his love so real, she forgave him his humor and accepted the embrace and one more kiss. "Love you, Eden."

She knew that even though he drove her crazy sometimes, it was the good kind of crazy. And she couldn't be happier. "I love you too. And maybe the lookout is a good idea after all…"

Epilogue

Eden sat on the front porch of their home outside San Antonio. The house had been finished for three months now. The porch circled the entirety. And in every way the place was like living a dream. Beautiful green country land spread out in all directions. The sky was as blue as ever and the weather now in Texas was perfect. Reid came out to join her. "It's early." He handed her a mug and draped a blanket over them both on the double swing.

Eden smiled, a sleepy, happy smile. "I couldn't sleep. The day is so gorgeous, I didn't want to miss any of it."

"How are you feeling?"

"Great." Her hand rested on the small bump that carried their new baby. "I think I was made for pregnancy."

His arm across her shoulders pulled her closer. "I think you were made to be right here."

She could only agree.

Vets 4 Life turned out to the most successful grassroots effort the country had seen in a long time. They had a map with pins all over the country. They were growing and building momentum every day. Now, congressmen contacted them about supporting bills instead of the other way around. And she had turned most of the daily running of the thing over to Nigel. He'd started dating someone and seemed happy to stay in DC forever. Which left her and Reid the freedom to do whatever they wanted.

He finished one more year of rodeo after the year they met. He went to worlds, made it to the winning blocks with a second place, and decided to be happy with that. Apparently, his small taste on her board had ignited some other fires in him. He started rodeo fundraisers, his own think tank, and a new business training guys to do rodeo. Every now and then, he went out to DC to help his dad on a tough case.

"Are the guys coming today?" She snuggled into him, yawning.

"Yep. For dinner. Kellie too. I'll get the fire going and the BBQ." He pressed his lips to the top of her head. "You falling asleep out here?"

She nodded. "I think so."

He scooped her up in his arms. "Then I say, we get back in that huge bed you had me buy."

"I'm gonna have to agree with you there, Mr. Browning."

"That's just what I want to hear from you, Mrs. Browning."

She smiled against his chest. "Do you ever wonder how we got to be so happy?"

The arms that cradled her close as they curled back into bed together were cozy, but the mouth that started a trail down her neck was anything but. As she turned to him and ran her hand up his back, his mouth covered hers and kissed her smile until she was well and fully focused only on him.

Prickly Pear Cactus Jelly

Ingredients:

27 Prickly Pears
1/4 C Lemon Juice
1 (1.75 ounce) Package Fruit Pectin
4 1/2 C Sugar

Directions:

Sterilize all jars and lids

Slice ends off of each prickly pear. (The fruit from the cactus). Make 1 long vertical slit down each one. Use the slit to hold the skin and peel off. Discard Peel.

Place peeled pears in a blender; puree in batches until liquefied. Press puree through a fine-mesh sieve set over a bowl. Discard pulp and seeds.

Measure out 3 cups prickly pear juice, lemon juice, and pectin into a large pot. Bring to a boil, stirring constantly. Add sugar and return to a boil, stirring constantly. Let cook, about 3 minutes. Remove from heat.

Pour prickly pear mixture into hot jars, filling to within

1/4 inch of the top. Wipe the rims of the jars with a moist paper towel to remove any food residue. Top with lids and screw on rings.

Place a rack in the bottom of a stockpot and fill halfway with water. Bring to a boil and lower jars 2 inches apart into the boiling water. (Be careful-use a holder) Pour in more boiling water if necessary to bring the water level to at least 1 inch above the tops of the jars. Bring the water to a rolling boil, cover the stockpot, and process for 15 minutes.

Remove the jars from the pot and place onto a cloth-covered surface several inches apart, and let cool at least 24 hours.

Check lids for sunken evidence they are sealed.

Pecan Pie

Ingredients:

1 baked 9 inch pie crust
1 cup granulated white sugar
1 cup light corn syrup
1 tsp vanilla
1 tsp salt
1/4 tsp cinnamon
4 eggs whisked
1/2 c butter
2 cups pecan halves (plus extra to decorate top)

Instructions:

Heat oven to 350.

Whisk together sugar, corn syrup, vanilla, salt and cinnamon. Add eggs and whisk until smooth. Melt butter until brown. Pour over sugar mixture and whisk to combine. Chop the pecans, then stir them into the butter and sugar mixture until combined. Pour the entire filling into the prepared pie crust. Line the top with extra pecans.

Bake for 40-50 minutes or until top is lightly browned. Pie will be ready to go once the top is puffed up into a dome which will sink once pie has set and cooled. Transfer to wire rack and let cool until it reaches room temperature.

Chapter One of Rough Stock

Read a sneak peek of *Rough Stock* here!

Chapter 1

Silvia Diaz kicked off her stilettos and closed her eyes. Thankfully, the lights had dimmed at the charity auction, and no one could see her. And her feet were under the table, so they stayed hidden.

Her brother, Axel Diaz, was the keynote speaker tonight. As well he should be. He'd been on the board of the Sports for Kids charity for years, and if that alone wasn't impressive, how about his stellar career as Major League Baseball's top shortstop? His playing for the pro baseball team the Seattle Sharks had brought Silvia and her mom to Seattle when she was a teenager.

Now, at the age of twenty-four, she was so over it.

Over all of this.

She knew she should be grateful. And she was.

She knew she should be proud of her brother. And she was.

She knew she should count her blessings about her mother's near cancer scare last month that had turned out to be benign. And she did.

But . . . Silvia had been living in her brother's shadow forever. At least, it seemed so. Ever since he started playing baseball, she and her mom had gone to most of his games. To support *him*. No matter what Silvia had going on, everything was dropped when her brother had a game. He'd then turned his success into supporting their family, which put him even more into the father role in her life.

Maybe if her dad hadn't left when she was two years old, then this all wouldn't have happened, and her brother wouldn't be acting like her dad all the time. Her parents could have been their son's number one support, and Silvia could have lived her own life, made a few decisions on her own, scooted a bit farther from the spotlight.

The audience began to clap, and Silvia realized she hadn't been listening to a word her brother had said. She focused on him now. His dark hair gleamed beneath the bright lights of the stage. His body, which was in top physical condition, seemed made for the tuxedo he wore. His olive skin set off the white flash of his teeth and his dark brown eyes—which mirrored hers.

His words were eloquent and heartfelt, and the audience was eating them up.

Silvia had no doubt tonight would be a record-breaking fundraising night for Sports for Kids. The charity raised money for underprivileged kids who wanted to play sports, but their parents couldn't afford it. Sports for Kids paid for team and uniform fees.

"You might think I'm here because I'm looking for a tax write-off," Axel told the audience.

A few chuckled. Everyone knew very well that wasn't the case.

"But the truth is, I was one of these kids."

Silvia had heard Axel's speech many times. She didn't remember her dad, and it used to bother her that Axel was so open about their family problems, but now, she felt numb to it. She'd stopped caring. Mostly.

"My dad's alcoholism turned him into a man no longer fit to be a father and husband," Axel said. "When he left my mom, me, and my baby sister, he took everything. The only reason I'm standing here today is because of the compassion, and the open wallet, of a Little League coach in Southern California."

The room erupted into clapping, and most of the audience wiped at tears in their eyes.

All right. So Silvia was moved as well. Who wouldn't be when hearing stories of her brother and these kids—kids who didn't always have enough to eat, either. She blinked back a stray tear on her cheek, then felt a pat on her shoulder.

She looked over at Brighton, Axel's wife. Her dark hair was swept into an elegant twist. Brighton smiled at her with sympathy, and Silvia smiled back. But inside, she was annoyed. She didn't want sympathetic looks or smiles. She didn't always want to be known as Axel Diaz's baby sister. Silvia wanted to be taken seriously. She'd finally gotten up the courage to tell her brother that she was dropping out of college—which he was paying for—because she wanted to go to hair school instead.

Or not. Truthfully, she didn't know. But staying one more week at the community college wasn't an option.

She'd already dropped her classes—though Axel didn't know that. Being surrounded by eager students who discussed test and quiz scores like they were debating a presidential candidate was so far out of Silvia's interest that she'd begun to develop anxiety about going to class. Not the normal stress of any other college student, but anxiety so crippling that some days, she stayed in her dorm all day.

Fortunately, she had her own private bedroom, and her roommates didn't much care if she was coming or going. They were caught up in their dating drama.

Speaking of dating . . .

Silvia slipped her phone out of her clutch to see that Darren had texted a few minutes ago. She hid a smile, since Axel was talking about how a twelve-year-old girl had gotten out of a bad home situation, and now played on a top club basketball team. It would look rude to be smiling during that story.

Hey babe, I got off work early. Can you meet up?

Her pulse thrummed at the invitation. Darren had finally started paying attention to her. He'd dated one of her roommates a few weeks back, but things were over between them now. Still, they had to keep their relationship on the down low.

I'm at a charity thing with my brother, and he's my ride.

The three dots on the text app danced for a few seconds.

Need a getaway car?

Her heart slammed into her chest. Should she? Did she dare?

I'd love one.

Send me a pin, babe.

She sent the pin just as she heard her brother say, "And

one of our volunteers at the office is here tonight. My sister. Silvia, will you come up and say a few words?"

Heads turned, necks craned, and people started to clap.

Silvia felt her heart drop to her stomach. Yeah, she volunteered once a week at Sports for Kids, but so did a lot of people. Axel had not warned her about this, and he knew how much she hated the limelight.

With trembling hands and an ultra-fake smile, she slipped her phone into her clutch. The last thing she wanted was for Brighton to see any texts from Darren. Another sore point with her brother and his wife. They were both freaks about who she did and did not date. Just because Axel had been known as "Cold Axe" before he met Brighton didn't mean Silvia had to stay home on the weekends.

The clapping increased, and Axel was waiting for her, his winning smile somehow not making her feel any better.

Silvia couldn't very well pause to put on her shoes—everyone was watching her now. Hundreds of eyes. Well, maybe two hundred pairs. But that was a lot. Really, a lot.

Brighton nudged her. "They're waiting for you, Silv."

Silvia swallowed, her throat feeling like the Sahara Desert. They *were* waiting for her. And they were still looking at her. Clapping. Smiling.

Her gaze connected with another man across the table. Grizz. One of Axel's best friends and former teammate at Belltown. Grizz was currently the all-time best catcher in the MLB, and his wife Rachel was next to him, all smiles. She'd been one of the top dancers in Chicago, and now she had her own studio, in addition to an adorable brood of three kids. No losers at this table. Except for maybe Silvia herself.

But Grizz wasn't smiling. His gaze was intent on her, his brow furrowed, his expression . . . concerned.

Could he tell she was about to have a panic attack?

No, no one could tell, because she wasn't going to have one. She was going to walk to the stage like a normal person, deliver a dazzling speech about how her life had been changed through her volunteer work, then escape with Darren for a fun, irresponsible night doing what twenty-something college dropouts did . . .

But she never made it to the stage.

Silvia stood and took a handful of steps before her legs turned to water. And her breath rushed out. Then the room spun.

Her last memory was of Grizz McCarthy's deep voice as his arms circled her. "Someone call 911."

Purchase your copy of Rough Stock and continue reading!

Read all books by Sophia Summers

JOIN HERE for all new release announcements, giveaways and the insider scoop of books on sale.

Cowboy Inspired Series
Coming Home to Maverick
Resisting Dylan
Loving Decker

Her Billionaire Royals Series:
The Heir
The Crown
The Duke
The Duke's Brother
The Prince
The American
The Spy
The Princess

Read all the books in The Swoony Sports Romances

Hitching the Pitcher
Falling for Centerfield
Charming the Shortstop
Snatching the Catcher
Flirting with First
Kissing on Third

Northbrook Hockey Elite Six Book Series

Vacation Billionaires
Holiday Romance

Her Billionaire Cowboys Series:
Her Billionaire Cowboy
Her Billionaire Protector
Her Billionaire in Hiding
Her Billionaire Christmas Secret
Her Billionaire to Remember

Her Love and Marriage Brides Series
The Bride's Secret
The Bride's Cowboy
The Bride's Billionaire

Copyright © 2021 by Sophia Summers

All rights reserved.

No part of this book may be reproduced in any form or by any electronic or mechanical means, including information storage and retrieval systems, without written permission from the author, except for the use of brief quotations in a book review.

Made in the USA
Las Vegas, NV
20 December 2023